INTO THE
WILD

DANIEL SMITH

This is a work of fiction. Names, characters, places, and incidents are products of the author's imagination or are used fictitiously and are not to be construed as real. Any resemblance to actual events, locations, organizations, or persons, living or dead, is entirely coincidental.

World Castle Publishing, LLC
Pensacola, Florida
Copyright © Daniel Smith 2016
Paperback ISBN: 9781629894300
eBook ISBN: 9781629894317
First Edition World Castle Publishing, LLC, February 29, 2016
http://www.worldcastlepublishing.com

Licensing Notes

Cover: Karen Fuller
Editor: Lisa Petrocelli

DEDICATION

For Albany, Ethan, Maddox, and Kaylea.

Acknowledgements

I would like to thank my family for their unyielding support and encouragement.

CHAPTER ONE

The logging road ran on for miles, winding and twisting through Erichson's Nature Preserve, in southern Oregon. The preserve had been set aside in James Erichson's will as a reminder of his logging legacy, as well as his sense of poetic justice. After his death in 1985, all logging operations in the area had ceased. Spots were now overgrown with weed and brush, and there was little evidence of it having been used in the last twenty-five years. The occasional litter on the ground was the only human trace on most of its seventy-five mile run.

"Can you believe this place?" asked Stacey, an exuberant twenty-two year old woman. She had the body of a dancer and long brown hair pulled up in a loose ponytail. Her hazel eyes reflected the excitement in her voice. "Ryan! Are you coming?" Her gaze was directed toward the woods surrounding the logging road.

"Yeah, I'm coming," Ryan muttered. Ryan was twenty-four, with blonde hair and blue eyes. He was at least twenty pounds overweight and out of shape from working in an office building most of his life, smoking a pack and a half of cigarettes a day. He stepped up next to Stacey and leaned over, placing his hands on his knees. He was out of breath and tired from the hike. Sweat rolled down his face, despite the cool morning temperature.

"You okay?" asked Stacey without looking over at him.

"Yeah," he said between pants. "Just a little winded."

"If you got out of that office once in a while," she said, "and quit smoking, you'd be able to do things like this."

"Yeah, yeah, I know," he muttered. He wiped his still-sweating face with the back of his hand and sighed.

"I'm serious!" she said, placing her hands on her hips and acting as though she were pouting. Stacey and Ryan had been dating for a couple of years. Stacey was content with how things were going, and Ryan wanted more. He had proposed to her, but she rarely wore the engagement ring. Secretly she was not entirely sure she wanted to be married. This had created a rift between them, and they were almost always fighting.

"Do you want to camp here?" demanded Ryan. "I don't want to walk all damned day!" He had caught his breath and was no longer sweating. He looked at her with an apologetic look on his face but saw that she had either ignored his jab or did not hear it. "Is this where you want to set up?"

"Nah, just a little further. I'm sure there's a creek running through here somewhere. That would be the best place to camp. At least that's what my dad used to say."

"Fine!" he said. "Gimme a minute, and I'll be ready."

She looked over and chuckled. She watched for a moment as Ryan looked around as if he had lost something. The look of confusion on his face was almost comical. His head darted back and forth a few times, eyes constantly moving.

"What are you doing?" she asked. "Did you lose something?"

"No," he said. "I thought I heard something a minute ago. Do you smell that? It smells like a skunk."

"It was probably a skunk then," Stacey said and laughed. "We are out in the woods, you know. Let's get a move on."

"Could be," he muttered. "Let's go." They set off, and soon Stacey was several yards ahead and walking at a steady, even gait. Her long legs easily crossed the rough logging road. She jogged three days a week and went to the gym regularly. Ryan hadn't exercised since high school, and it showed.

Ryan trailed behind, huffing and sweating. He walked at a steady pace as well but was unable to close the gap. He could not catch up, but he wasn't falling behind either. He kept up the pace and focused on not tripping.

Stacey stopped in the middle of the road, and Ryan finally caught up to her a moment later. She stood stone still, a content look on her face while she observed her surroundings. She happily looked around the logging road, and the sound of water running could be heard not too far off in the distance.

All was silent for close to a minute, then a shrill scream echoed throughout the woods. It sounded like a person in a cheesy horror movie screaming.

"What the hell was that?" asked Ryan. He had a smug look on his face.

"I don't know," Stacey said, rattled. "It sounded like it was right behind us."

They strained to hear but heard nothing. The silence was palpable, and even the typical background noise of the nature preserve had gone deathly silent. Not even the birds made a peep.

They listened for well over five minutes without hearing another noise. They started up again, still hiking into the heart of the nature preserve. The sound of birds slowly started again and soon created a lilting backdrop of sound.

"I think we ought to stay closer together," Ryan said at length. Stacey quickly nodded in agreement. She walked slower, knowing that Ryan would not be able to match her pace. They walked side by side along the logging road, silently.

After several hundred feet, they came to a narrow stream and followed alongside it for several hundred yards. The logging road continued through a large clearing. Remnants of dozens of past campsites dotted the clearing every few feet. Forgotten chairs, shoes, and overflowing garbage cans cluttered the area. It looked as though each camper left something behind.

At five hundred feet square, the clearing was very large. The only thing living in the clearing was scrub plants with saplings less than waist high. There were large areas where past campers had made campfires and pitched tents. Piles of firewood, bought at the gas station near the edge of the nature preserve, were stacked near some of the long-abandoned fires.

"This will work for a campsite," Stacey announced, regaining her usual cheer. "Let's set up here."

Ryan slid his pack off his shoulders and removed the rolled tent. He opened the drawstring bag and dumped all the contents onto the ground in a jumbled heap. He set to the task and was soon sweating and cussing, unable to set the tent up properly. He struggled with the tent for quite some time, checking the instruction sheet every few minutes. Sweat dripping down his face and cursing under his breath, he stared at the sheet, trying to find an unwritten trick on it.

Stacey busied herself with gathering a small

pile of kindling and some good-sized dead branches, and she had a workable campfire going in no time. She used some of the dry firewood sitting around their campsite.

"I'm struggling here," he announced. He finally walked away from the tent, lit a cigarette, sat down heavily, and smoked. By the time he snubbed out the cigarette, he had calmed down. He stood with a grunt and walked over to the tent, finally ready to finish it.

"Need help, babe?" Stacey asked.

"No!" he shouted. "I've got this!"

"Okay." She sighed. "It looks like you're getting frustrated, that's all."

After another ten minutes of working on the tent, and with much less cursing than the first time, he drove the last tent stake into place with an overdramatized grunt and flung the mallet off to the side. "There, finished!"

"You did great!" she said as he walked over and plopped down next to her and stretched. He gazed into the fire, lost in thought.

"Now what?" he asked. "It's about an hour before dark, and everything is done. You were right, this is kind of relaxing. Unless you count that damned tent."

"Yeah. I wish you still played guitar," Stacey said absently. "You could have brought your acoustic and played it out here! That would have made the night nice."

"Yeah," Ryan answered. "After the band broke up and the crap that Craig pulled, it didn't seem worth it anymore. Granted, I always loved playing out. Too bad the last gig we played was ruined because that asshole Craig took our pay and bolted. I miss being in a band sometimes."

"I always thought he was shady," Stacey offered. "Not sayin' I told you so."

"Well, I—" he started but was interrupted by a second bloodcurdling shriek, but this time it was much, much closer.

"That was just on the other side of the stream," Ryan said, pointing. "Just inside the tree line."

The breeze carried a putrid smell like rotting meat and damp carpeting to their nostrils.

"Ugh, what's that smell?" Stacey said, her nose wrinkling.

"I don't know," Ryan said and bolted to his feet. He pulled a hunting knife out of the backpack and took it out of the sheath. "We should get into the tent."

They ducked into the tent, now on its second camping trip, and zipped the door flap. Stacey unzipped a window and peered through the gray mesh. At first, nothing stirred in the clearing. After several long, tense minutes of watching, Stacey gasped.

"I don't hear any birds or crickets, or anything," she whispered.

"What?"

"I don't hear any birds," she repeated. "Before, on the logging road, we heard tons of birds, now listen. There are none! It is stone silent. It's actually kinda creepy."

"So," he muttered. "Big deal."

"It's just that there should be birds," she said softly, "and there aren't any."

The sound of something moving through the trees interrupted their conversation. Stacey watched as the trees nearest to the stream began to thrash. Suddenly, a loud cracking sound followed by a sharp grunt echoed across the clearing. A tree trunk, seven feet long and about eight inches in diameter, seemingly flew across the small stream. A second tree was flung to the ground.

A shadow passed across the fabric of the tent's ceiling.

"Duck," Stacey screamed, dropping to the floor of the tent. Ryan looked up just in time to watch the fabric rip over his head. A large shape loomed over them, peering down.

The smell they had noticed earlier filled the tent. An odor of putrid meat, wet fur, and skunk combined to make both occupants gag. Their eyes watered from the odor, and both clamped their hands over their mouths and noses.

A large hairy hand reached into the shredded tent and grasped Ryan by the arm. A soft grunt sounded as the arm hoisted Ryan up as if he were a small child. The next thing Stacey heard was Ryan screaming, then she felt a spray of warm, thick liquid, and everything went dark.

***

The world began to materialize slowly. Stacey looked around as the fog lifted. She was surrounded by three large, purposeful-looking men. All three wore black tactical gear, and one was wearing a black ball cap.

"Ma'am are you alright?" one of the men asked. "Are you hurt?"

"I think so," she said. "Who are you, where's Ryan?" She could feel the first fingers of panic constricting her chest. She jerked her head back and forth. "He's my boyfriend. We came here for a camping trip. The last thing I remember was hearing him scream."

"I'm sorry, ma'am, your friend's gone." he said. "Let me explain. My name is Jackson, Bert Jackson. I'm head of outside security for H.C. Wiln Corporation. We have a facility in the area, and the fence is not too far off. We're out here to make sure that no one trespasses."

"Okay. So what happened to Ryan?" Stacey asked, slowly coming out of her daze. She looked from one face to the next, seeing nothing but the eyes of hardened men. She looked down at the spattered blood now drying on her clothes.

"He's dead. It looks like he was killed by some kind of wild animal," Jackson said, "Rumor has it there's a Sasquatch in these woods. In fact, at one point I had heard that our scientists had caught one and were studying it. If that's the case, it may have escaped."

"For all we know, there may be a serial killer loose in the woods," another shorter man piped up. Jackson shot him a look that required no words, causing the man to fall back into silence.

Stacey stared at the man blankly. Her face carried a far-off look, as if she was looking straight through the assembled men.

"Tell you what," he said. "How about I take you to my office, and we can arrange a trip to town for you. We'll cover everything for...did you say his name was Brian? Ryan?"

"Ryan," Stacey said as tears began streaming down her cheeks. "His name is... I mean *was* Ryan Penn. He sold insurance. He wanted to go see his family in Iowa."

"Come on," Jackson said gently and guided her to a waiting utility vehicle, a passenger body on an ATV frame. A logo depicting H.C. Wiln and the word "Security" across the back side of the vehicle.

Stacey sat in a backseat as the vehicle started and drove on the logging road. She began to sob hysterically, her hands covering her face.

A radio crackled to life. *"Jackson, report."*

"Male is dead, KIA. Female is en route to facility," Jackson responded into the handset radio. "Please advise."

"Copy that," the voice answered. *"Volunteer*

Corp for her."

CHAPTER TWO

"Don't worry about it, babe," Bethany Edwards said, setting a cup of coffee in front of her husband Mike. "You'll find a steadier job." She turned and walked over to the counter, putting cereal into a bowl and pouring milk over it. She poured a cup of coffee for herself and carried her mug and bowl to the table.

"Yeah," he said. "Since I got out, we've been struggling." He paused to take a sip of coffee. "Either way, I've still got the crew, and I'm pretty sure I can downgrade to a volunteer when I get a steady job."

"Mike, we're struggling, but it's on our own terms," Bethany said. "Besides, it's getting easier all the time. Remember just last year, running out of diapers was enough to make us count change. Now we have a little in the bank. We'll be fine."

"It would still be great to pay all the bills every month," he muttered.

They sat at the kitchen table in their cramped two-bedroom apartment. The bills had been piling up since Edwards had been discharged from active duty with the US Army. While he was deployed, Bethany and Abigail had lived with her parents.

Abigail, their two-year-old daughter, sat in her booster chair eating her breakfast of Cheerios and blueberries. She was wearing a T-shirt with a rainbow on it and a brightly colored barrette in her curly blonde hair. A bright pink tutu finished off her look for the day.

"Ever since I've gotten back and we moved out of your parents' house it's been rough," he said. Mike Edwards was six feet tall and around one hundred eighty-five pounds. He had light hair and green eyes. He had served in the military as an infantry medic. "It sucks—I've applied to every ambulance service in this part of the state, and no one is hiring. I could always find a job in a factory or on a fishing boat or something."

"It'll get better," Bethany said, brushing a curly brown hair away from her greenish-brown eyes. "What time do you have to go in today?"

"I have to be there around nine, and I'm on till the end of the week," he said. "I doubt we'll have much to do, though. Might have to save a kitten from a tree."

"It's work, though," Bethany said, "and Jefferson pays you well. Don't complain. It doesn't work for you." She walked over and kissed his forehead. "You could be stuck in a factory or working some go-nowhere job. At least this is what you want to do with your life. I want to go back and finish college, but I have no idea what I want to study."

He sipped the coffee in deep thought until a blueberry rolled across the table in front of him. He picked it up and rolled back in the direction it came from.

"Whatcha doin', bug?" he said.

"Daddy, hungry!" she said and giggled uncontrollably.

"Dad's not real hungry, kiddo," he said. "Dad's still waking up." A smile crept onto his face as his daughter's squealing laughter continued.

"Well, Beth, at least the firehouse ain't bad work," he said at last. "And it is a little safer than my last gig. I like it, and that's what counts."

"Yeah, and sometimes it's better the devil you know," Bethany said.

"You want to hear something dumb?" he asked, glancing at the clock. "I miss the structure. Not the patrols and all that crap, but I miss the structure and having a set schedule."

"Yeah, well, if you don't get a move on, Jefferson'll blame me for you being late again," she said with a smile. "Structure!"

He stood, carried his mug to the sink, and walked back over. "I love you girls, see you later!" He walked to the door, grabbed his phone, wallet and keys, and pocketed them. He grabbed his bag from its spot near the kitchen door. Edwards got into his old pickup truck and drove off.

Passing through the small town of Deer Ridge, Mike was still amazed by the lack of traffic. The town was home to less than fifteen thousand but had a strong small-town feel to it, something that he and Bethany loved. He drove toward the fire station, the old truck shuddering at stop signs. He pulled into the parking lot behind the fire station and backed it into a spot across from the door.

Edwards slipped the transmission into first gear and shut the truck off. He opened the door with a long creak, then walked across the lot and went inside.

"How you doin', Mike?" asked Bill, one of the senior guys at the fire station.

"Not bad, Bill," Edwards answered. "Anything going on?"

"Nah," he answered. "Is Abbey still having those nightmares?"

"No, cutting out sugar before bed worked great," Edwards said. "That was some great advice."

"Glad to hear it," Bill said, scratching his bulging stomach. "Jefferson posted a meeting for you guys coming on shift, so stow your gear and get to the conference room. I think he's already here. Somethin' about smoke jumping."

"Gotcha," Edwards said. He walked to his

locker, dropped the bag on the bottom shelf, and slammed it shut. He locked the padlock and slid the keys back into his pocket. He walked down the hallway, passing doors to the bunk rooms before rounding the corner to the conference room.

Seated at the far end of the table was Jefferson. He was reading pages in a file folder and ignoring everything around him. Glancing at his watch, Edwards saw that he was twenty minutes early.

Elliot Jefferson was captain and rarely called meetings. He was forty years old, trim, and average height. He shaved his head to disguise a drastically receded hairline and had brown eyes that smiled more than he did. A drooping handlebar mustache hung past his chin and made him look older.

"Mike! How are you?" he asked in his booming voice, eyes leaving the page he was reading for less than a second. "There's a packet of information in front of all the seats, if you want to read it now."

"Doing good, cap," he answered and sat down in one of the chairs facing the door. He stretched and was rewarded with a hearty pop from the middle of his back. "Feeling pretty good this morning."

"As soon as the other guys get here, we can start this meeting," Jefferson said at length. "Grab some coffee if you want it. Jones should be bringing doughnuts."

Over the next ten minutes, the majority of the crew filtered in, some discussing sports, others walking in silence. Nearly every man had shown up by five minutes to nine. All the seats around the table were filled except one.

"Is everyone here?" asked Jefferson. He looked around and saw that there was only one man missing. "Looks like Kennedy is making his own schedule again," he said shaking his head.

This brought a groan out of all the men at the table.

The door flung open, and Kennedy bound through it. "How you all doing?" he shouted. "You should have seen the chick I picked up last night!"

"Since Mister Kennedy decided to join us on time, I think we can get this meeting in gear," Jefferson said. "State is asking for volunteers again, for smoke jumpers. How about it, any hotshots in the room? They'd like seven guys."

"I'll do it!" Edwards said, raising his hand.

"There'll be some parachute training," Jefferson said and watched another couple of hands go up. "It pays better!"

Kennedy raised his hand and grinned. "Sounds like fun."

"That'll work, guys," Jefferson said. "Training will start in a few days."

He stood and walked out of the room.

"Hotshot training, huh," said Jason Kennedy. "I used to be a logger, so I figure that should come in handy. Besides, it should be a little more exciting."

"Yeah, right," Edwards chided. "I've known you for almost as long as I've known myself. You're in it for the women!"

"You caught me, Mike," Kennedy said, feigning surprise. "That's why I'm doing it. Everything I do is to impress women. Oh, wait!"

Kennedy was six feet two inches tall and two hundred pounds. He was built like a football player and regularly worked out. His dark hair had a natural curliness to it, and he kept it short. His brown eyes always had a tinge of mirth to them, and his smile was often contagious. "Besides, I bet the chicks'd dig it when I tell 'em I'm a smoke jumper!"

"I was a medic overseas and I've had parachute training, so I think I'll be an easy fit," Edwards said. "And since they let all kinds into this outfit, I'll be stuck keeping our ass out of trouble, as usual."

"Cool, ought to be fun," Kennedy muttered. "I can always use a wingman."

The men on shift went about their day, seeing to all the minor tasks needed to keep a firehouse running smoothly. The daily chore list was divided up, each man assigned a household chore.

Edwards was in the process of cleaning the bathroom when his phone dinged. He checked it to find a new text message. He opened it and read the words from his wife: *Call me when you can, Abbey's bedtime.*

He dialed her number and waited as the phone

connected.

"Hey, Babe," Edwards said into the Blackberry. "What's up?"

"Abbey wants to tell you good night," she said, and called Abigail over to her. "Go ahead."

"Hey, kiddo, Dad loves you!" he said into the phone.

"Hi, Daddy!" she squealed.

"You head to bed now, baby girl," he said softly. "Sleep good."

"Love you, Daddy," she said. He heard her footsteps as she ran away, giggling.

"She's such a cutie," Bethany said, "but she is a little wound up. How's it going?"

"I volunteered for a hotshot crew," he said. "I'll probably be a medic and a smoke jumper."

"That's awesome!" she said. "What's the training like, and what kind of pay is it?"

"The training won't be that bad since I've been through it all before, and the pay should be more than what I'm making now," he said.

"That doesn't sound so bad," she said. "I told you things would get better."

"Yeah," Edwards said. "Should be pretty cool. Besides that, Jason is going to be there, too. Anyway, I got stuff going on. I'll talk to you later."

"Okay, love you," she said as she hung up.

Edwards sighed and walked to the bunk room. He was getting ready to lie down when the alarm went off. Everyone was a blur, bodies moving in all directions.

Several men pulled on Nomex suits, and others were preparing the trucks. Drivers were being informed of where they were going.

"Edwards, get a move on, you're with me," Drew shouted. "A semi rolled on the highway."

"Hoo-ha," he grunted. He grabbed his kit and jumped into the back of the ambulance. He stowed the bag and settled into the passenger seat. Drew, the driver, shifted the transmission and pulled out of the fire station.

Drew was a paramedic and had seniority on the ambulance crew. Edwards had the same amount of experience and training. Jefferson acknowledged this by putting the two men on the same pay scale. Drew got to call the shots, and Edwards didn't argue.

The fire engine and tender truck left the station's lot, followed closely by the ambulance. With sirens blaring, the column raced through the evening dusk. Unconsciously, Edwards pulled the dog tags he still wore out of his shirt and kissed the heavy steel cross attached to the beaded chain. He had done this same action on every op and every ride-along he had done with the cavalry division to which he was attached. It started out of nervousness but had become a natural action when he was preparing to do anything stressful.

"Don't need to do that, kid," Drew said. He had noticed Edwards kissing the cross. "This is a cakewalk."

"That's what I thought, last op I was on right before my tour was up," he said. "We were patrolling a barren stretch of road, and we were attacked by insurgents. They had snipers on the ridge above us and RPGs directly ahead of us."

"Oh yeah," Drew said as he drove. "What happened?"

"Our column was hit," Edwards said. "Out of six vehicles, one came out intact. We lost quite a few men that day. Half of the guys, experienced cavalry and armor division men, said it was a cakewalk. There wasn't enough of the men in the lead vehicle to put into a Ziploc bag."

"Yeah," Drew said. "But this is a semi in a ditch, not a patrol through hostile territory."

Chapter Three

"Great job, guys. I know the last two weeks have been pretty rough, what with the daily jump training and all, but good work! I got the team position roster typed up," Alex Jones said as the men of his group gathered at the end of training. "Atherton, Burnside, Barton, you three are general duty men. Kennedy and Patterson, you're sawyers. We got some nice chain saws for you boys. Edwards, you, of course, are our medic, and I'm team leader. Any questions? Kennedy, before you ask, you will have to cover the general duty stuff when there is no chain-sawing to do."

Kennedy lowered his hand just as quickly as he had raised it. A smug grin spread over his face, but he remained quiet.

"Alright, boys, before we go any further, I want to thank Kennedy and Edwards for helping out with the training. You guys are the head of the class. Gold stars for both of ya. Now, this is what we've been training the last couple of weeks for. Got a report of smoke, possibly fire in Erichson's Nature Preserve in the northern part of the state."

"Prob'ly some dumb-ass hiker," said Kennedy. A chuckle rippled through the room.

"Enough," said Jones. "That is true, there are always hikers in that region, lots of camping. There also might be a damned hippy commune and an ashram for all I care. There is smoke, so we are heading out to investigate. It's been a dry-ass spring, and the winds have been pretty steady in that area. Perfect scenario for a wildfire. Time to earn our keep."

All the men gathered in the meeting room muttered in agreement. It took all of five minutes for the chatter to die out.

"Alright, guys, I'll give you some time, make your phone calls. Tell your families you love 'em, and you'll see them all soon! We'll meet back here in about a half hour," Jones said. "Once we're back here, we'll mount up."

Edwards pulled the battered Blackberry out of his pocket and dialed. Walking through the firehouse, he found a quiet spot, sat down, and hit the send button.

"Hello?" Bethany answered in a sing-song voice.

"Hey, I just got word, we're heading out on a wildfire," Edwards said into the phone. "We'll be leaving in about half an hour. Erichson's Nature

Preserve—someone called in some smoke. Got to go and check things out."

"Hopefully it's nothing," she said. He could hear the worry in her voice. "I'll let Abbey know what's going on."

"Thanks."

"Be careful," she said.

"Sure will. See you in a few days," he said and disconnected. He locked the keypad and slid the phone back into his pocket.

Edwards walked out to his old truck and was waved over to where Kennedy was standing. He was smoking a cigarette and drinking an energy drink. He had just slid his cell phone into his pocket, a wide grin on his face.

"Hey, Mike," Kennedy said, taking a drag. "You ready for this?"

"Of course," Edwards said. "You know me, always ready." He walked to his truck and reached inside. He pulled the duffel bag out and set it down on the battered hood of the truck. Opening it, he retrieved a blue and purple silicone band, slid it onto his left wrist, and positioned it just above his watch.

"What is that?" Kennedy asked.

"Abbey gave it to me the other day," Edwards said. "I think it came with a kid's meal from somewhere."

"Cool," Kennedy said. He glanced at the watch on his wrist. "Everything'll be fine, dude. Just going to fly out there and take a peek. Real easy day. Plus, we'll get hazard pay for this."

***

Edwards sat on the wooden bench in front of the lockers, duffel bag at his feet. It was six minutes before "wheels up," and he was anxious to get moving. He was wearing his work uniform, a pair of dark blue EMT-style scrubs tucked into his worn and battered logger boots. His dark blue polo shirt showed the blue star of life on the right shoulder and an American flag on the left. He pulled the ball chain and kissed the cross, and then tucked it back into his gray T-shirt. His Nomex sat in a neatly folded pile on the bench next to him. His first aid kits and other gear had already been loaded.

"You alright?" asked Kennedy. "You look a little pale."

"Just a little preflight jitters," Edwards muttered. "I'll be fine."

"If you say so," Kennedy said. "It won't be that bad—fly up north, bust some dumb-ass hiker for burning some wet wood, then come back home. Easy money!"

Edwards looked at Kennedy and was opening his mouth when the old public announcement system crackled to life, cutting off Edwards's comment before it even began.

"All hotshot personnel, report to the north lot. All hotshot personnel to the north lot," the dispatcher said.

"Let's go," whooped Kennedy, running out of the locker room. "Oh yeah!"

Edwards stood and walked out of the locker room, duffel bag on his shoulder and Nomex under his arm. He arrived in the north lot in time to board a city bus and ride to the airfield.

"Can I get your attention for a minute, guys," shouted Jones. It took a moment for everyone to get settled and look up at him. "That's better. Now then, this is our first op as a hotshot team, but it ain't our first rodeo together. We've all got relevant experience, but you also gotta learn from the experience of others. Remember, a team is only as strong as its weakest member."

This statement started a round of murmurs around the bus.

"All I'm saying is that the only thing that can beat us is us," Jones finished. He turned and sat down in his seat. "Stay vigilant, and remember your training."

"Let's go!" he told the driver who eased the bus into the driveway and pulled out of the parking lot.

It took five minutes of driving before the bus came to a stop at the airfield. The group disembarked and got onboard the plane. The modified Douglas DC-3 was idling just outside the hangar. Of the original twenty-one passenger seats, eight had been removed, and sleeping berths had been bolted to the bulkheads. The berths had been donated by a fishing boat owner after the renovation of one of their better-appointed vessels. Each bunk was just under six feet long and had a thin mattress pad and a light fixture. In all, there were eight sleeping berths and thirteen passenger seats numbered zero through twelve. Jones, the team leader, claimed seat number zero and let everyone else sit wherever they pleased.

Edwards stowed his duffel bag in the cargo compartment and took a seat. The seats themselves had also been upgraded, straight out of a luxury jet, and featured cup holders and various dials and switches. There were USB plugs in all the seatbacks and a mesh pocket to hold a cellular phone or tablet. A flat-screen monitor rounded out the upgrades.

Edwards was trying to get comfortable when the intercom crackled. *"Eh, this is your Captain, Elliot O'Toole, speaking. I am joined by my lovely assistant, Mister Colin McDunnin. We are currently cleared for takeoff,"* O'Toole drawled from the cockpit. *"You will notice that we are the most luxurious airline money can buy, as our interior upgrades have been fully installed, but I regret to announce they are not yet functional. If you wish to lean your seat back, you must first slide your knees forward and lean back. Our electrical is next on the agenda, but as none of the nonfunctional systems are safety related, implementation will have to wait."*

"So what, that means no in-flight movie?" quipped Kennedy. A slight chuckle ran through the group.

"If you all will buckle your seat belts, we will be

getting underway," O'Toole announced. The big plane eased onto the tarmac. *"Please observe the no smoking signs, and place your trays in the upright locked position."*

Edwards waited until he felt the big plane's angle change, then he unbuckled his seat belt. He walked over to a sleeping berth and swung up onto the top level. He dozed off as soon as his head hit the mat.

CHAPTER FOUR

"Mike, dude, wake up," Jason Kennedy said, nudging his shoulder.

"What?" asked Edwards.

"We're about ten minutes out, kid," Bob Crenshaw said. "Hate for you to miss your big chance to slap a hippy for dropping a joint into a pile of kindling."

"Yeah, your prob'ly right. I wouldn't want to miss that." Edwards laughed. "Thanks, Bob."

"No problem, kid," Bob grunted. "Hey, you ever see an oil drill? A'course ya did, you was over in Iraq, weren't ya?"

"Afghanistan, Bob," Edwards said as Kennedy chuckled.

"Whatever, one sand trap is like all the others," Bob said. "I almost went to Iraq back in '91, you know. Anyway, we passed one o' them oil drills on the way in a few minutes ago. Said Wild-Co or some damned thing on the side of it. Ever hear of 'em?"

"No, can't say that I have," Edwards said. He slid out of the cramped bunk and swung his feet to the floor. He walked to the cargo compartment door and stepped through. He looked around until he found his duffel bag but could not find his Nomex.

"Jason, what the hell did you do with my Nomex?" shouted Edwards.

"What are you talking about, dude?" he asked. "I ain't seen it."

"You must have, I had it sitting with my duffel bag," Edwards shot back.

"Alright, that's enough!" Jones shouted. "This is our first time out as smoke-jumping hotshots. Watch your asses out there. I sure as hell ain't going to bury any of you anytime soon. That being said, we'll be over our drop in about five minutes, so gear up."

He walked to the cargo compartment door. "Hey, genius, your Nomex is on the rack with the rest. Gear up."

"Thanks, boss, I must have set it down when I got on board," Edwards said with a shrug.

"I expect you to be first in line at the door. You're a natural leader, and with your prior training, this should be easy," Jones said. "Maybe even help some o' these other guys. Mikey, you've had more jumps than any four of these other guys put together. Except for Kennedy. He's nuts, though."

"Sure thing," he said. "I'll do my best."

"Do that, and be sure to be the first at the door," Jones said, rubbing a hand across his forehead. "Don't want anyone at the door who'd freeze up. When it's time to jump, I know you won't freeze. I don't feel comfortable pushing a guy out of an airplane. Hell, I barely feel comfortable jumping out of a plane myself."

Edwards nodded, hustled to the rack, and leafed through the Nomex until he found his and pulled on the bibs, then the coat. He pulled the parachute onto his shoulders and cinched down the straps. He pulled his helmet on and tightened the chin strap, then packing the rest of his gear in available pockets, pouches, and straps, Edwards felt ready. A quick glance around the cabin told him that the rest of the crew was ready as well. Edwards walked to the door and attached the carabiner on the end of his static line to the overhead cable. He stood next to the door and glanced at his watch.

"*One minute,*" drawled the pilot. "*Please note the exit directly to your right, and ah... mind that first step, it is a big one.*"

"Pop the door, thirty seconds out," Jones said. "Watch for my signal!"

Edwards pulled up on the handle and slid the door toward the rear of the fuselage. He glanced at his watch and noted that it was nearly two o'clock.

Reaching up, he pulled the goggles down over his eyes and waited.

Suddenly, the plane lurched. O'Toole watched as the altimeter gauge began to spin around randomly. Both engine tachometers redlined, then dropped to zero. Craning his neck, O'Toole saw that the left side propeller was still spinning. He could still hear the engine droning.

"Colin, take a look out your window," O'Toole said laconically. "Is that prop still spinnin'?"

McDunnin looked out the window, twisting in his seat. "It looks like it is."

The sound of metal screeching across metal erupted from the right side engine nacelle, followed by a gout of flame. The propeller slowed and stopped, smoke billowing from the engine. He looked out at the propeller and saw that it wasn't turning. He pulled hard on the controls, trying to even it out.

"Shit!" McDunnin shouted. "I think we're in trouble."

"Eh, this is your captain," O'Toole said over the PA. "We are having some engine trouble. Strap in, I'm going to try to set her down easy."

The sudden uneven deceleration caused the plane to lurch to the right, knocking Edwards off balance. He fell out of the door, pulled the static line taut, and popped his parachute. Edwards tumbled, which caused his chute to tangle above him. He knew that he would never survive the fall if he didn't stop his spin, so he reached out for the release handle. He pulled, cutting the main chute away. Flaring out, he slowly started to regain control when the treetops rushed up to meet him. He panicked and clambered for the reserve chute release handle. The last thing he remembered was his fingertips brushing the handle.

Chapter Five

Edwards groaned and opened his eyes. He was hanging from a tall oak tree, his reserve chute tangled in the high branches. He uncinched the straps, dropped to a nearby branch, and lowered himself to the ground.

Looking around, it didn't take him long to get his bearings. A thick pall of smoke curled up from the woods a mile and a half northeast of this current location. He pulled the helmet off and clipped it to a carabiner on his parachute harness.

"Shit," he muttered. "Jones, Kennedy, do you copy?" he said into his radio, he listened for a full minute. He twisted the volume button all the way to the off position, then fully on, just to be certain it was on.

"Jones, Kennedy, anyone," he said again. "Anyone got a read? I am down, repeat, I am down and en route, advise."

Edwards listened as his radio crackled softly.

He heard a series of low cracks and the sound of something being dragged. He began to walk toward the rising smoke. "Any smoke jumper got a copy?" He glanced at his watch and saw that the face was shattered and the hands had stopped. He pulled the parachute harness off his shoulders and dropped it next to the tree where he had been stuck.

He trudged, silent, toward the smoke, hoping to find the rest of his team. It seemed as if the woods were growing closer. A dark feeling gripped at his heart as the radio silence grew heavy. He was not prone to panic, but he could not shake the uneasy feeling.

Edwards began to notice a few broken branches on the ground here and there. As he continued, the fallen branches became less scattered with bits of broken aluminum among the branches. The further Edwards walked, the larger the debris he saw on the ground. He tugged the cross out and held it to his lips, uttering a short prayer under his breath.

Less than a quarter of a mile away, he saw a fragment of a wing, complete with the engine nacelle. He tried his radio again and was rewarded with silence.

He picked up the pace to a jog and saw that the last quarter mile was less strewn with debris. He entered a small clearing and was awestruck by the sight that met his eyes.

There, at the far edge of the clearing, the

Douglas DC-3, both wings ripped off, was resting against a large Cyprus tree. There was a ragged gash just behind the cockpit, and the entire tail section just aft of the passenger compartment lay at an angle seventy-five feet away. The span between sections was strewn with debris of all kinds. He was shocked to not see any bodies among the wreckage. The smell of spilled aviation fuel filled the air, but the downed plane was not on fire.

It took Edwards a full minute to process the sight before he jumped into action. He ran to the downed plane and ducked inside. He paused at the door, waiting for his eyes to adjust. He listened for any sound, but all he heard was silence.

The passenger compartment was empty. Edwards noticed a spot of blood on the deck. He walked toward the cockpit, ducking under the jagged aluminum hanging down into the walkway. He looked into the cockpit and saw blood on every inch of the control panel. Both the pilot and copilot were dead. O'Toole had been pinned. The control panel had crushed down onto his legs, nearly severing both of them, and cut the femoral artery. Edwards estimated that he bled out in under two minutes.

The copilot, Colin McDunnin, was not as lucky. The control panel had pinned him as well, but not enough to sever his limbs. His struggling had caused the edge of the control panel to cut into his thighs superficially. His right arm had been broken, a compound fracture of the radius. The blood loss from the pale bone piercing through the flesh of his forearm had stopped bleeding prior to his death. Minor cuts and scrapes covered both men's' faces. The windshield had shattered in, peppering the men as the plane went down.

Edwards was mortified to see a single gunshot wound in the back of the copilot's head. He stepped out of the cockpit and off of the plane.

He leaned over, bracing himself by putting his hands on his knees. As he was looking down and trying not to be sick, he noticed a group of footprints overlapping in the soft soil of the clearing. The prints circled around the plane, then led off into the woods. He cautiously followed the prints into the woods, his head on a swivel every step. He had walked less than one hundred yards when he froze in place.

A squirrel chattered at him from a nearby tree. Edwards peered around, searching for anything that stood out. Satisfied that nothing and nobody was out in that part of the nature preserve, he continued to walk. He followed the trail of footprints until he stumbled into a second, smaller clearing. The sight that greeted his eyes made his blood run cold.

There, lying facedown in a row, were five of the men of Edwards's hotshot crew. He waked over to the first man in the row and saw that his hands were bound behind his back, and he had a gunshot wound in the back of his head. He glanced at the rest of the men and saw the same thing. All their hands were bound, and all had been shot in the back of the head from point blank range.

"They were executed," Edwards muttered aloud. Backtracking to the crash site in a daze, he entered the separated tail section of the DC-3. It took a moment for his eyes to adjust to the low light.

He searched for close to fifteen minutes until he found his duffel bag. Opening it, he checked the display on his cell phone.

He found the screen completely shattered. Tossing it off to the side, he checked the other duffel bags and found that the other phones had either been broken from the crash or the battery was completely discharged.

He dropped his bag and removed first his Nomex coat and bibs, then he took the EMT-style cargo pants and the polo shirt off. He pulled on a pair of carpenter-style jeans and a green flannel shirt over his gray T-shirt. He pulled on an insulated vest and relaced his logger boots. He laced the Ka-bar he had worn in Afghanistan onto his belt and stuffed his work clothes and Nomex back into the duffel bag, then tossed the useless duffel bag against the bulkhead and ignored it.

Passing into the next room of the tail section, there were several bins lining the walls filled with gear for nearly any mission the hotshot team would have. Edwards grabbed an IFAK, an individual first aid kit, and a full-sized medical pack. He stuffed both into a nearby backpack. Checking other gear bins, he found a Pulaski ax and a handful of protein bars. A little extra digging produced a wide mouthed water bottle with an internal filter and a basic survival kit, all of which went into the backpack. There was a map sitting on the floor. He scooped it up and looked at it. Taking the pen out of his pocket, he marked an X on the map where the plane went down, as well as the location of his teammates. He folded the map and slid it into a pocket on his vest.

Edwards pulled a pair of rubber gloves out of his bag and slid them onto his hands. He entered the cockpit and gently closed both men's' eyes. "I'm sorry, guys. I'll make this right."

Edwards exited the plane and followed the trail through to the clearing with his murdered teammates. He knelt beside each man and closed their still-open eyes and stood over them a moment. He balled the gloves up and tossed them to the ground next to the dead men. Kissing the cross around his neck, he heaved a heavy sigh. "I don't know who the hell did this, but I'll find a way to make the bastards pay."

Edwards set out on his new mission and continued through the woods until he hit the logging road. Once there he pulled out the map and followed the logging road as it wound throughout the nature preserve like a snake. Pulling out the GPS unit he had found in the backpack, he tried to turn it on, only to find that it too had a dead battery. He looked around to get his bearings, and then with shaking hands he put the useless unit back into the pack and continued moving forward on the logging road. He had only walked for only a few minutes when he stopped and leaned against a fallen tree.

"Son of a bitch," he muttered. "They're all dead!" He just stood there with tears running down his face for several long minutes, then he sank to the ground and sat cross-legged. He couldn't fight back the rush of emotions as he sat and cried.

Finally, when he had regained his composure, he pulled the handkerchief out of his pocket and wiped his eyes and nose. He stood and forced himself to continue to follow the logging road. His thoughts strayed as he walked.

He remembered Jason Kennedy, his best friend since kindergarten. They grew up less than three blocks apart and were closer than brothers. They had been in and out of trouble for years and had even served in Afghanistan together.

He remembered the rest of the guys who for the most part had adopted him into a large extended family. Most of the older guys would give him advice about anything and everything. Whether Edwards wanted the advice or not, the guys gave it to him.

When he took the job at the firehouse, Jones had told him, "Listen, kid, we're like a big, messed-up family. Little Abby just got herself a whole mess of uncles!"

A tear streaked down Edwards's face as he continued to walk. He occasionally lost his footing, and stumbled, but he barely noticed. He trudged on, his misery sustaining him, and the monotony of the walk prevented him from thinking too hard. One thing tugged at his thoughts—he had not seen Kennedy among the executed smoke jumpers.

Chapter Six

"Come off it," said the woman laughing. "It'll never happen!"

"Just one date," the man said. "We can just take a walk around town."

"You sure know how to show a girl a good time," she said rolling her eyes and walking away. She purposefully added a little extra swing in her hips as she walked.

"I'll call you," the man called after her. "I love you," he added softly.

She walked through a door and shut it behind herself. The door plaque read "Holly Andrews, Corporate Lawyer." Holly sat at her desk and checked her e-mail. Her eyes darted back and forth across the screen, reading. Her phone rang, and she picked up the receiver.

"Holly Andrews," she answered. She toyed with a wisp of her hair while she listened.

"Ms. Andrews, what have you come up with

on allowing Wiln mine to operate in the nature preserve?" a voice asked.

"Mr. Schuester, I have done everything I can think of and even made up a few tricks. They just will not allow it," she answered.

"I'll just have to send a man out to grease some wheels. Make the park service see things our way," Schuester said. "Keep me posted."

"I certainly will," she said and hung up the phone. She pulled a phone out of her shirt, punched out a text message, and hit send. She slid the phone back into her cleavage and checked her other cell phone, a smartphone that the company supplied.

Being a corporate lawyer for the H.C. Wiln Corporation, a worldwide mining, energy, and electronics conglomerate, kept Holly busy. She had a workload that required nearly fifteen hours of work a day. The company had provided her with a live-in office and no dress code. She had a pair of assistants at one point in time, but she had run them off. Her bedroom was adjacent to her office.

Holly was attractive, with long, strawberry-blonde hair, blue eyes, and a supermodel body. She was smug in the security of being attractive and wasn't afraid to mention it.

Her selected work uniform for the day was a pair of khaki shorts that showed the perfect amount of leg, pink minimalist running shoes, and a button-down shirt with a strategic number of open buttons.

The men of the Far North Facility and offices followed her every movement. She knew that nearly every woman there hated her, and all the men wanted her.

She felt a pressure against her chest and checked the display on the phone in her shirt. "Good work, keep it up." The display showed a number, but no name.

Replacing the phone, she stood up. She locked her laptop and left the office, walking toward town, a self-enclosed shopping complex at the center of the H.C.Wiln Mine Far North Facility.

The town carried everything from cigarettes and chewing tobacco to iced coffees and women's lingerie. This allowed the facility to be operated round the clock by a completely live-in crew. Shifts were twelve hours for operations and eight hours for the R and D department. A tour was generally thirty days, and the pay was at the top of the scale. The workforce was very content with the arrangement.

"Hey, Holly, whatcha needin'?" asked the clerk behind the counter. His eyes crept from the top of Holly's head to her feet and back, staring at her, making her slightly uncomfortable.

"Hi, Murray, just stocking my fridge," she replied, forcing herself to be upbeat. "Ever get any more iced mocha?"

"Sure did, about ten." He winked with an

innuendo-laced smile plastered across his face.

"Oh, Murray, I'm much better than a ten!" She giggled. She leaned over, placed her elbows on the counter, and squeezed her arms together.

"Ah, yeah, of course you are," Murray said. "I got your iced coffee in, it's in the cooler. Anything else you need?"

"No, I should be fine for now," she said, gathering her iced mocha and a few other things. She signed for them again, giving Murray a cheap thrill by leaning her elbows on the counter to sign the sheet. She put her hands on either elbow, her arms framing her breasts, and squeezing them together. She knew the charges would never make it to accounting, and she was okay with that.

Holly carried her bags back to her office and loaded the fridge. She attempted to initiate a Skype call with a contact labeled D, but was dejected to see that D was off-line. She quickly composed an e-mail, checked her phone, and set about reading the first of a series of revisions to the corporate operations and research department handbooks. She sipped an iced mocha and sighed.

CHAPTER SEVEN

Edwards lost himself to the walk and soon had traveled nearly two miles away from the crash site. He continued following the logging road, and he felt better as the hours wore on and the distance between himself and the downed plane grew.

Edwards walked throughout the afternoon and into evening. When he could no longer see his feet, he decided it was time to stop and try to sleep, and barring that, at least wait out the night. He walked fifty feet into the woods and dropped the backpack. He laid down, resting his head on it.

"At least it's early in the season," Edwards muttered aloud. He was relieved that there were no mosquitoes yet. He stared straight up at the dark canopy of treetops and thought about his friends and family. Eating a quick meal of a protein bar, he washed it down with a swallow of water. He dozed for over an hour but was unable to sleep soundly, waking several times, each time looking at a darkened sky. Each time, he laid his head back onto the pack and shut his eyes.

The sun had begun to creep into the sky when Edwards stood and pulled the backpack on, and then continued his trek. After nearly an hour of walking, he stopped at a crossroad. His sorrow began to catch up with him for just a moment, and he forcibly shook it off.

The logging road continued curving toward the north. A pair of shallow ruts, possibly from an ATV or small pickup truck, branched to the east, carving a path through the brush.

Edwards stood, looking at both possible routes, and analyzed them as best he could. The logging road looked to not have been heavily traveled in years, whereas the ATV trail seemed fresh. The footprints in the mud seemed to mill around, then continue to follow the smaller rutted-out path. He shrugged and followed the ATV trail. After walking several hundred feet, he came to a stream. He saw several footprints crossing all directions, intermingling with the ATV path. He studied the path in front of him for nearly a full minute.

After walking for another couple of hours, he stopped, ate a protein bar, and drank the rest of his water. He filled the bottle from a nearby stream, making sure the filter was set up correctly, then sat and looked around.

With a sigh, Edwards stood and started to move again. He noticed that the sound of birds, a constant background noise, started to fade, then suddenly stopped altogether. Edwards strained his ears, trying to figure out what had caused the sudden silence.

The soft sound of thrashing branches caught his attention, causing Edwards to whip his head around. Subconsciously holding his breath, Edwards tried to ready himself for anything. His hand drifted to the handle of the Ka-Bar on his hip.

A raccoon bumbled out of the brush and waddled across the ATV path. It paused and peered at Edwards, then ambled away.

"Mike, pull it together," he murmured. "It's just a damned raccoon."

Shaking his head, Edwards pressed on, and after walking another hundred and fifty feet, he came upon a large clearing. There was evidence of people camping, and many had left their mark of either garbage or camping equipment they had neglected to take with them. Off in the distance, Edwards saw an undisturbed campsite.

Crossing the clearing, Edwards walked up to the tent and seeing no fire burning, he got a closer look at the tent. The fabric was torn in several places, and the door flap hung open. He stuck his head inside, then withdrew it quickly. The interior of the abandoned tent reeked of blood and human waste.

He glanced around the tent's perimeter and noticed dozens of prints around it. His blood ran icy cold when he saw the largest of them. The prints were huge, over eighteen inches long, barefoot, and very deep.

"What the hell made those, Bigfoot?" Edwards mumbled. He began following the prints, walking through the woods, unsure of what was waiting for him, but he was prepared for anything. The weight of the Pulaski ax over his shoulder did more to reassure him than the Ka-bar strapped to his hip.

Soon he approached a narrow, hard-packed pathway. The path was a little wider than the one he was following but seemed to be more traveled. He followed this new path for over forty-five minutes before he started to wonder where he was going. He nearly ran face-first into a large steel gate.

He stepped off the path, melted into the trees, and listened. He heard voices off in the distance. He knew that the odds were good that they had killed his team, and they were only a couple hundred feet ahead of him.

Chapter Eight

In the dark, a deep groan emerged followed by a cough. A second groan followed the cough.

"Where am I?" the voice asked. "What the hell hit me?"

"You're a new member of Volunteer Corps," a trembling female voice answered. "My name is Stacy, and I've been here for about four days."

"I'm Jason Kennedy, and I'm a smoke jumper. My stick was winging our way to Erichson's Nature Preserve to investigate a possible wildfire."

"I see," Stacey said. "Let me help you up." She walked over, her bare feet slapping on the cold concrete floor. She grabbed his hand and pulled him into a sitting position.

He took a deep breath and sat a moment. His head was spinning, and he felt as if he had been hit by a bus. Swallowing hard, he took a deep breath and steadied himself.

"Stacey, can I ask you a question?" he said. He

winced as pain ran through his body. He fought a wave of nausea, raising his hand to his mouth and wiping it with his palm.

"Sure, Jason, go ahead."

"Are there lights on in this room?" he asked.

"Yes, there are," she answered after a moment. She stood, and he heard her walk across the room and nervously tap her hands on the wall. He sensed that she was uncomfortable.

He raised his hands to his face and felt the bandages wrapped around the top part of his head. He felt around the bandage, trying to find the end of it. He soon grew frustrated and huffed.

"Why is there a bandage on my head?" he asked.

"That is a difficult question to answer," she replied. "The guys that volunteered you are nothing more than thugs. And they have a Sasquatch. Not sure how, but they have a Sasquatch."

"Bullshit," he retorted. "They don't exist."

"I thought so too, until I witnessed one kill my boyfriend," Stacey said, growing silent for a moment. "Let's wait, the doctor will probably be here in a little while to check you out."

Kennedy slowly stood, easing his way to the nearest wall, counting his partial shuffling steps as he did. He slowly eased his way back into a sitting position with his back against the wall and leaned his head against it. He did the math and figured out the rough dimensions of the room.

"I'm sorry," he said, "about your loss."

"Don't be, I've cried nonstop for days. I feel terrible saying I'm over it, but I don't feel anything about it anymore. I just want to get out of here."

"Not too sure what help I'll be with my eyes bandaged shut," he said scratching his shoulder. He acknowledged at that point that he was naked. He cleared his throat, but Stacey cut him off before he had a chance to say anything.

"Everyone brought to Volunteer Corp is stripped naked. They want to be sure no one will hang themselves," she explained before he could ask. "Plus, I think it's a way to keep us in line and give the guards a cheap thrill."

"I see... Actually, I don't, I—" he started but was interrupted by the sound of a heavy steel door sliding open. The sound of three sets of feet walking through the door caused Kennedy's head to turn toward it. He balled his hands into fists by his sides but felt powerless, his shoulders slumping.

"Hello, my volunteers, I am Doctor Russel, but ya'll can call me Doc. Since that's out of the way, let's get you checked out, my big, strapping firefighter man." He had a soft voice with a cultured southern accent. A moment of silence followed after he entered the room.

"Kennedy. My name is Kennedy."

"Okay, okay, no need to get pissy," Doc said.

He walked over to where Kennedy sat and began to unwrap the bandages. He slowly and methodically rolled the thick cotton, oblivious to any concept of time. After several long minutes, he finished and clicked his tongue.

"Looking good, my handsome friend," he said softly. "The bandages were a formality. Your left orbital socket was fractured badly. There was a possibility of severe trauma to your eye, up to and including blindness. Do you remember anything after the crash?"

"No, nothing, what happened?" Kennedy asked, his edginess apparent in his voice.

"You, my friend, were attacked," Doc said, relishing the dramatic pause he created. "Our Sasquatch worked you over pretty well. I took the precaution of injecting you with some of our fancy medic nano-bots. Right now, as we speak, they are repairing the soft tissue damage and helping to rush the bone to mend itself. They're rebuilding your face. Isn't that just peachy?"

Kennedy said nothing, just stared straight ahead, his eyes moving slightly in every direction. His gaze stopped on one of the guards standing in the doorway. "Hey, Lumpy, give me a cigarette!"

The guard looked at him contemptuously until Doc nodded at him. The guard complied, shaking a cigarette out of his pack and holding it out to Kennedy. He lit it for him, then walked back to the doorway.

"Thanks," Kennedy muttered.

"When they brought you in to me, you were in pretty rough shape. Your left eye was obviously damaged, sunken, and the area around it—your orbital socket—was badly swollen. You were covered in blood, and they were sure you were going to die. All that is taken care of, and in a day or two, you'll be right as rain."

"There is no way a Sasquatch attacked me," Kennedy said, ashing on the floor. "They don't exist."

"I beg to differ. We captured one and injected it with a different design of nano-machines," Doc said. "Those kind allow us to control it. Most of the time, he is allowed to roam the nature preserve, free as a bird, but when we need him, all we have to do is whistle."

"That can't be ethical," Stacey said, angry.

"I don't know and don't really care," Doc said, an edge creeping into his voice. "I'm paid to do a job, not debate ethics with you. I actually have an assignment for you, young lady, so if you'll come with me and leave our firefighter friend to recover, I—"

"Wait," Kennedy stammered. "I, uh…need her help."

Doc stared at Kennedy, and Kennedy stared back at him from his right eye.

After nearly a full minute, Doc threw his hands up. "Fine, you can keep her for now." He turned and walked through the door. "I'll be back for her in a day or two, so don't get too attached. Although I can't blame you for wanting to keep her, she is a...fine specimen. If you're into that." The doctor chuckled to himself as he walked out of the room and into the hallway. The door slammed shut behind him, and Kennedy sat silently as the locks were relocked.

Kennedy raised a hand to his left cheek and felt around gingerly. He felt an almost unperceivable rippling under the skin. He brought his hand away and saw thick white fluid on his fingertips.

Stacey walked over and threw her arms around his neck. She pressed her body against his and squeezed him tightly. He wrapped a brawny arm around her slim body. He heard her breath catch in her throat.

"Thank you," she said, her voice barely above a whisper. "How's your eye? I mean, can you see?"

"Yeah, I can see okay," Kennedy lied. He had full vision in his right eye, but his left eye was just a gray haze. "We need to see if the guards can get me an eye patch or something...so it can heal properly. It's still a little sensitive to light."

She nodded and sat down, wrapping her arms around her knees. She sighed and leaned her head on her forearms.

He looked at her and closed his left eye. He noticed the scared expression on her face, the lithe dancer's body, and the long hair pulled back away from her face. She had big brown eyes and a slender nose, and a pretty face despite the nervous smile.

"Stacey, can I ask you a question?" Kennedy asked after a moment.

"Sure," she muttered. She lifted her head and looked at him sitting against the wall a few feet away. She smiled, despite herself.

"What do you do for a living?" He took a long drag off his cigarette and snubbed it out on the floor.

"I'm a dancer in Seattle," she said. "I teach at Miss Bellachek's Ballet Studio. I also work part time as a receptionist at a nursing home."

"I see," he said nodding. "Your husband, what did he do?"

"We weren't married. We weren't really even engaged," Stacey said, a hint of sadness in her voice. "In fact, we had broken up about ten times in the last year and a half. Anyway, he was working his way up in an insurance company. So, Jason, what do *you* do?"

"Like I said before, smoke jumper, hotshot crew. I'm also a career firefighter," he said. "I worked as a logger for a few years. Started when I was eighteen but quit shortly after I spiral-fractured my ankle."

"How did that happen?" she asked, wide-eyed.

"Working, clearing a blown-down hillside. There were dozens of logs, and I was rigging the cables. My foot got caught, and my dumb-ass crew boss didn't know where I was," he explained. "He signaled to the man at the controls at the top of the hill to pull the cable up. I was dragged a hundred and seventy feet by my left foot. I was in the hospital for six weeks. I have two plates, six pins, and thirteen or fourteen screws in my ankle."

"So what, you quit logging after that?" she asked.

"Kinda. The company I worked for took care of all the medical bills, and the owner was willing to keep me on," he said smiling. "Until I beat the living shit out of that crew boss on my first day back. I was a logger for about five years. I did a few odd jobs, did a little traveling, I served awhile in Afghanistan, and then I fell into firefighting."

"My boyfriend wanted to visit his family in Iowa, and I insisted we go on a camping trip." She teared up and sniffled. "It's my fault he's dead."

"It's not," he said. "You were in the wrong place at the wrong time."

He looked down at his wrist for the first time and was delighted to see that his watch was intact and still worked. He wore a rugged dive-style watch on a two-inch-wide leather band. He and Edwards both had the same band. Edwards's wife Bethany found one and bought it for him, and when Kennedy saw it, he went out and bought one just like it.

"It's four o'clock," muttered Kennedy. "We

need to figure out a way to get the hell out of here."

"I'm not sure what's going on, but the people that were here when I was brought in were drugged or something," Stacey said. "All they did was sit. They sat and stared straight ahead. It was terrible, ten naked people just sitting there. I was wide awake and moving around and everything. It was the longest day of my life. I cried nonstop for the first three days."

"Let's try the door," Kennedy said and stood. He teetered for a moment and regained his balance. "If they kept these people drugged, maybe they're lax about locking the door."

He hobbled toward the door, favoring his left ankle as he walked. He turned the door handle, but the door was still locked. He rapped his fist against it softly.

"Dammit," Kennedy said. "Okay, new plan. Uh, bang on the door and yell for help. When a guard comes to the door, get him to open it."

"How?" she asked.

"Tell him I'm having a seizure or something. When the door opens, we'll knock him out." Then he added softly, "Hopefully, he's alone."

She began to bang on the door. There was no window, but there was a narrow slot that slid open. Kennedy stood alongside the door.

"More frantic," Kennedy said. "You got to really sell it!"

"*Help! Guard!*" she screamed, banging as hard

as she could.

The slot in the door slid open a few inches. "What the hell do you want?" demanded a gruff voice.

"This guy is having a seizure, I think. He started to shake then fell down, and...oh, God, please help him!" She was breathing frantically, and tears were running down her face.

The slot banged shut, and the lock slid open. The heavy door lurched outward. A single guard stepped into the doorway and looked around. Kennedy's huge hand grasped the security guard's collar and dragged him into the room.

"What the hell?" demanded the guard as Kennedy's fist slammed into his face. A quick jab to the midsection doubled the guard over, and a hard-rising knee crashed into the man's forehead.

He crumpled, landing in a heap on the floor. Kennedy crouched down and pulled the man's coat off.

"What are you doing?" Stacey asked as Kennedy was unbuttoning his white uniform shirt.

"If we wander through the halls naked, it may draw some attention. Especially a hot little number like you," he said winking. "We can split up this goon's clothes and hopefully find a locker room, or maybe even our own clothes in storage or something."

Stacey nodded, blushing, and walked over. She helped Kennedy undress the unconscious guard.

He handed her the guard's button-down shirt and boots. He pulled the guard's work pants on and pulled the handcuffs off the duty belt. He cuffed the man's hands behind his back and tossed the belt into a corner.

The white shirt came to the middle of Stacey's thighs, and the boots were way too big for her but too small for Kennedy.

"Aren't we a pair," she said and smiled. "Let's get the hell out of here."

Kennedy stuck his head out into the hallway and looked first one way, then the other. When he was satisfied no one had seen him, he stepped out of the holding cell. "Come on," he whispered.

Stacey stepped out into the hallway and leaned against Kennedy's shoulder. "Which way?"

"Uh, how about that way?" he said, pointing. "There are some doors over there, maybe one of them is a locker room."

CHAPTER NINE

Mike Edwards crouched alongside the ATV trail for what felt like an hour although he knew it had been less than a minute. Sweat dripped down his forehead, despite the chill in the air. The voices ahead of him faded, and the woods around him went silent again. He waited an additional couple of minutes, then stepped out onto the path again. He cautiously walked forward on the trail, curious where it was leading.

Edwards soon approached another clearing, this one roughly the size of a football field. The trail he was following bisected the open ground at about the mid-point. All around him, there was evidence of supply drops. Broken pallets stacked on the far side of the area, scraps of pallet wood, and parachute fabric littered the ground. Hundreds of footprints covered nearly every inch of hard-packed dirt, and the occasional cigarette butt was visible on the ground.

A cold wind kicked up, and from Edwards's vantage point, the sky was overcast and gray. He skirted the edge of the open field, staying within sight of the edge of the clearing.

It took Edwards a moment to notice, but at regularly spaced intervals stood stadium lights. With a series of heavy thunks, the lights began to kick on, casting the field in dazzling white light. He stepped up his pace and was soon running. He made it to the opposite end of the clearing and was back on the ATV trail. He continued to jog and had followed the path for almost half an hour when he stumbled onto a second, smaller clearing.

At the far end stood a low, cinder block building about the size of a two-car garage. It had two bay doors and a smaller main door.

In front of the building was a guardhouse with a traffic gate across the path. The gate blocked access to the building. The entire area was encircled in a twelve foot high chain-link fence topped with razor wire.

As Edwards was studying the clearing, he watched as one of the bay doors rolled up and several men exited the garage. They crossed to the guard shack and opened the gate.

From where Edwards sat, it looked as though all of the men—about a dozen—had a handgun in a holster on their belts, and a few carried assault rifles.

The sound of ATV's starting filled the nearly

silent woods and snapped Edwards's attention back to the garage. The two machines raced toward the larger clearing, and the rest of the men stood just inside the gate. After several long minutes, they began to relax, and many lit cigarettes, all of them beginning to chat idly. The sound of several different conversations drifted to Edwards's hiding place.

Edwards waited. The sound of a plane droning off in the distance alerted him. The men milling about looked up, and then most continued their conversations. A moment later, the plane passed overhead and disappeared into the distance.

Edwards returned his attention to the group and counted eleven men, whereas before there had been an even dozen, not counting the ATV riders. One had gone missing. Looking around, he strained his eyes struggling to see in the fading light and locate the wayward guard. The sound of a person passing through the woods less than twenty feet away from where he was caused Edwards to freeze.

The sound of a zipper, a faint whisper against the backdrop of sounds, caught Edwards's ear. Edwards hefted the Pulaski ax and crept over to the spot he heard the noise, not more than ten feet away. He could hear the sound of water hitting the ground and determined that the man was facing away from the clearing.

The noise of the ATV's, each one dragging a

pallet behind, shattered the silence and served to mask the sound of Edwards's movement. He spotted the guard and approached from behind him.

"What the hell, can't a guy even take a pi —" the guard managed to say before the side of the eight pound ax crashed into the side of his head. The guard crumpled, knocked unconscious.

"Nighty-night, Goon," Edwards muttered. He crouched and checked that the man was still breathing, and satisfied, pulled his coat off. He slid it on over his own clothes and zipped it up. The guard was easily fifty pounds heavier than Edwards, and the coat draped off of his hundred and eighty-five pound frame.

Edwards crept stealthily through the woods and eased his way into the fenced-in area. Walking toward the gate, he paused in the woods, watching as the men started to filter back into the garage.

"Anyone lock the shack?" a voice called.

"I'll check," a second voice called.

"Stay there," the first voice called. "Your relief will be there in a couple of hours. Gonzales wants the perimeter guardhouses staffed for the season."

Edwards watched as a man entered the guard shack and sat down. He stood and hustled toward the gate in plain sight. The guard at the shack stepped out and waved.

"Get lost again, Bill?" he asked.

"Yeah, I guess," Edwards muttered in reply.

The bay door had finished closing, and the final creak caught Edwards's attention for a split second, long enough for the guard to draw his sidearm and aim it at Edwards's chest. He raised his hands above his head.

"Who the hell are you, and where is Bill?" he demanded.

"Let me explain," Edwards said and lowered his hands. "You see…" he said. He scratched his chin and exploded into a football tackle, catching the guard at the knees and slamming his head hard on the ground. Edwards scrambled into a defensive position and saw immediately that his opponent didn't move. He moved over and saw the unnatural angle of the man's right leg. The grimace on the guard's face told the tale.

"Sorry, dude," he said, scooping the handgun up off the ground. He dropped the clip out and pulled the slide back. "That's the second time I've nearly been killed today." He tossed the gun into the woods behind him, and the clip was thrown in another direction.

He pulled the cuffs off the man's belt, cuffed his hands together, and dragged him into the guard shack. He sat him in the chair, and propped his leg up.

"This is going to hurt like a son of a bitch," Edwards warned as he pulled the broken leg back into position. A hearty snap told Edwards that the bone edges were lined up, and he wrapped the leg with a bandage he found in the first aid cabinet hanging on the wall. He used a rifle, sitting behind the door, and improvised a splint from it.

"There, now shut up," Edwards said, and used the rest of the bandage material to cover the guard's mouth. He rifled through the desk and discarded several empty cigarette packs and chewing tobacco tins. He tossed a pair of empty disposable lighters into the trash can and slid the drawer shut, then he noticed the key rack on the wall behind the desk and eyed a set with a label marked "Master Set," and plucked it off the wall. Stuffing it into his pocket, he turned his attention on the still-struggling guard in the chair next to him.

A quick search of the pockets and pouches revealed a handcuff key and a tactical-style ink pen with a screw-open compartment. Inside was another cuff key. Edwards quickly pocketed both items and left the guard shack. He crossed the clearing and circled the cinder block building. He approached the man-sized door and tried turning keys from the master key ring in the door locks. After the third or fourth try, the handle turned and he eased the door open.

Edwards stepped into the darkened room, holding his breath and waiting for alarms to blare at him. After a minute of no alarms, and no armed guards appearing, he silently exhaled. Detecting the faint smell of small engine exhaust lingering in the garage, he looked around and saw nothing. Neither of the ATV's he had seen earlier was inside.

After a moment, Edwards noted that the center section of floor, an area that was twenty feet square, was steel diamond tread. The rest of the floor was concrete.

Edwards chuckled. "Hopefully that's an elevator."

Starting at the entry door, Edwards worked his way around the garage, searching for either a man-lift, controls, or a set of stairs. Fifteen minutes into the search, he stumbled onto a false wall hidden behind an old refrigerator. He entered the door and found a stairwell. Easing his way down the stairs, he soon entered a dark hallway. Opening a nearby door, he was relieved to find a storeroom.

Shelves lined the walls and climbed from the floor to the twelve foot high ceiling. All manner of items were present—rounds for the guards' weapons, various grocery items, toiletries, clothing, and other things filled the shelves.

It took Edwards a moment to realize he was in a pre-inventory storeroom. He opened the door and looked at the placard to the right. It read "Dry Goods, Pre-count, Storeroom One".

He left the storeroom and searched for a better hiding place when the sound of a door at the end of the hallway swung open.

"We're starting at room one and going through it fast today," a voice said. "Not really feeling it right now."

The lights clicked on as Edwards shut the door. He waited near the back of the room as the sound of footsteps drew closer. He looked around and saw that he was in a nearly identical storeroom to the first one he was in, except this one was empty. He sat down on the floor and waited.

He unlaced his right boot, threaded the cuff key onto the lace, and retied his boot, making sure the key was under the laces as he was tying it. The tactical pen was slid into the IFAK on his belt. He smiled knowing he had access to a handcuff key if he needed one.

The door handle of the room he was sitting in began to turn, causing Edwards to jump to his feet. He crept silent and swift to the door and prepared for the worst. There was nowhere to hide, save for the shelving itself, but he planned to use the door as a temporary advantage by taking up a position on the hinged side. He held his breath, waiting for the door to open, Ka-Bar in hand.

CHAPTER TEN

Jason Kennedy, along with Stacey Cartwright, stepped into the hallway slowly and cautiously. Stacey hung back and waited for Kennedy to give her the all clear signal.

"C'mon," Kennedy said. "It's clear." Stacey bound over to where Kennedy stood and looked up and down the hall. She stood very close to him, her shoulder touching his upper arm.

"Which way?" she asked.

"Not sure, I'da taken better notes if I wasn't unconscious and essentially blind," he quipped. "Uh, let's try that way," he said and pointed.

They walked down the hallway and came upon a door. The placard next to the door read "Volunteer Corps."

Kennedy tried the handle and was relieved to find it unlocked. They stepped inside and latched the door behind them. Looking around, they saw that the storeroom held very little in the way of supplies. There were boxes on the shelves labeled with various names, and in the center of the room was a long steel table. A box labeled with Kennedy's name sat in the center. Stacey, having found her name on the end of a box, pulled it down. She opened it, pulled her own clothes out of it, and started getting dressed.

"You found your clothes," Kennedy said smiling. "You look almost as good with them as you do without." He winked at her, causing her to blush. He opened the box with his name on it and started to pull his clothes out. He saw that they were shredded and covered in blood, a result of the Sasquatch attack. He did, however, put on his own undergarments and socks. He pulled the guard's pants back on and laced up his sixteen inch high logger boots, tucking the bottom of the pant legs into them.

"Need some taller boots?" Stacey asked, laughing. "I've got some very fashionable knee-high ones at home."

"Nope, I need 'em for the support," he said. "It makes it easier to walk with this rebuilt ankle of mine."

She stared at him a moment.

"My own clothes are destroyed from the Sasquatch attack," he said. "Let's see if there's anything worth a damn in these other boxes."

She pulled a box down and opened it. Inside was a thick flannel shirt, a black T-shirt, shredded jeans, and a pair of black canvas shoes with white rubber soles. She pushed the box over to Kennedy, and he looked through it. He put on the black T-shirt, pulled tight across his broad chest, then the flannel shirt, and pushed the box aside. They looked through a few more and found a coat and gloves that would fit Stacey.

"At least we'll be warmer," she said with a smile on her face.

"Yeah, that is a bonus," Kennedy said, patting the pockets of the flannel shirt. He pulled out a partial pack of cigarettes and blue plastic lighter.

"Sweet," he muttered and casually lit a cigarette. "Let's see what else we have here." She looked over and wrinkled her nose at him. He shrugged.

The next several boxes contained nothing useful, but the fifth and sixth ones they checked had a bottle of water and some granola bars.

"Here, Stace," he said, exhaling a stream of smoke. "Eat this, you'll feel better."

He slid one of the granola bars across the table toward her. She picked it up and tore the wrapper open and bit into it hungrily.

"I didn't realize how hungry I was," she said with a mouthful. Her hand shot up to her mouth, and she giggled.

"Here," he said, offering the bottle of water, but he pulled it back just as she reached for it. "This is all we have right now."

She took the bottle and sipped gingerly, despite her gnawing thirst.

"We need to get moving," Kennedy said. He snubbed out the cigarette in the middle of the steel table.

CHAPTER ELEVEN

Edwards held his breath as the door handle slowly turned a little further.

"Hey, dude," a voice called. "Storeroom one is this way!"

"Oh, that's right," a second voice said, and the door handle returned to its original position. "It's already been a long day. How many more storerooms do we have to count?"

Edwards placed his ear as close to the door as he dared and strained to listen. The sound of voices and footsteps receding down the hallway was faint, but he heard it. He breathed a sigh of relief, and resheathed his Ka-Bar.

When he cracked the door open, he glanced out into the hallway, and satisfied that no one was approaching, he eased the door open and stepped into the hall.

Glancing over his shoulder, Edwards hugged the wall and moved quickly toward the stairs at the end of the hallway. There was a large hanging sign that illustrated the location of all the exits on the floor.

"All security personnel," an overhead speaker crackled, "Report to Vol-Corp. All security report to Volunteer Corps. There has been an escape."

Edwards heard a door open and close behind him and nonchalantly glanced in the direction of the sound. He saw a large, hunched man walking in his direction. The man's face was scruffy, and his nose showed the signs of having been broken at least once.

"Come on," he said gruffly. "Gotta get those damned volunteers wrangled up."

Edwards nodded and fell into step with the other man. Edwards kept his head down and walked with a rapid step.

"You know, this crap usually don't happen," the guard said. "Them Vol-Corp guys used to keep the volunteers doped outta their gourds."

"Oh yeah?" Edwards carefully remarked.

"Yeah, since that new doctor took over, they don't do that no more," the guard said. They walked in silence for several minutes until they reached the stairwell. They quickly descended several flights of stairs. The guard pushed a door open, and Edwards followed him into the hallway. A large sign hung from the ceiling with the words "Welcome to Vol-Corp" stamped across it.

"You check the storeroom, I'll take the holding

cells," the guard ordered. "Alright?"

Edwards grunted in approval and turned on his heel. He strode down the hall and found the storeroom with little problem. He pulled the door open and stepped inside. He looked around and noticed the same configuration as the other two storerooms he had visited. At the center of the room was a long, stainless steel table, and there were several boxes sitting out.

Edwards looked at the boxes and noticed the names on the end panels. There were several names he did not recognize. He found the one marked with the name "Kennedy, J", and his hopes rose. He overturned the box on the table and searched through the contents.

"Shit," Edwards whispered when he saw the tattered and bloody clothing. He pawed through the rest of the items and was relieved to not find Kennedy's logger boots. He noticed the nearest box had the name "Cartwright, S" scrawled across the label, and he glanced at it. Sitting on top was a bright pink wristwatch with a cracked face.

Edwards looked through the box and noticed that there were no shoes or clothing in that one either. The rest of the personal effects definitely belonged to a woman.

After a quick check of the other boxes, Edwards was sure Kennedy and this woman were alive somewhere.

"Only you, Jason, could find a woman in the

middle of a secret facility in the woods," Edwards muttered. He noticed that there were clumps of dirt, presumably from Kennedy's boots, on the floor leading to the door. Edwards followed them to the stairwell and down, taking the stairs two at a time. He whipped around the landing, followed the next flight of stairs down, and paused. Another flight of stairs descended, and a door with a card reader stood guard over the next floor. Edwards stood a moment scratching his chin and looking around. He noticed a small clump of dirt on the second step leading further down.

Edwards calmly walked down the stairs and pushed the door open at the next landing. He took three steps inside the door and coughed loudly four times.

"Son of a bitch!" A door flew open. "Mike! I thought you were dead, dude, I saw you get thrown out of the plane," Kennedy said as he stepped into the hall.

"Yeah," Edwards said. "I saw—"

The sound of a door slamming shut in the stairwell caused both men to look behind Edwards.

"Let's get out of this hallway," Kennedy said. "It's a little, ah, exposed for my tastes."

Edwards nodded and followed Kennedy into the office and helped him push the couch against the door. Edwards plopped onto the cushion. A heavy sigh escaped his lips.

"So, what the hell happened, Jason?" Edwards

asked. "You look like shit."

"If you think I look bad, you should see the other guy's fists," Kennedy grinned. "You're looking pretty beat yourself. Well, at least I have one hell of a story. I got my ass kicked by a Sasquatch."

Edwards stared at Kennedy for a full minute.

"I'm serious," Kennedy said. "It gets better—there's a nut job doctor running around, a real weirdo. He told me he injected me with nano-bots."

"Yeah, okay," Edwards said skeptically, "and I'm the king of England!"

"Well, when I woke up, I was essentially blind in my left eye. Right now, I can almost see." Edwards stared at Kennedy and saw that his left eye had a grayish haze over it.

"Wait," a female voice interjected indignantly. "You told me you could see!"

"Yeah, well, it calmed you down, didn't it," Kennedy snorted. "A frantic woman would make this escape impossible instead of just incredibly unlikely."

The woman crossed her arms and looked away.

"Jason, you clod," Edwards blurted, sensing the tension. "You haven't introduced me to your friend."

Stacey stood and crossed the room. She elbowed Kennedy as she walked past. "My name is Stacey Cartwright," she said with a dazzling smile.

"I'm a dance instructor in Seattle."

"Mike Edwards," Edwards answered. "Paramedic. I've heard this clown's story, how'd *you* get here?"

"My fiancé and I were hiking in Erichson's Nature Preserve and had just set up our camp. To make a long story short, we were in the tent when we heard a noise. After that it gets kind of jumbled. I remember the tent being ripped open and a giant hand, and then it goes blank for a while. Then nothing, until I woke up in the volunteer room crying."

"I see," Edwards said. He stood and stretched. "Here's what I'm thinking. These guys are up to some pretty nasty stuff. They're willing to kill to keep people away from this facility. Hell, I got shot at right after the plane went down."

"Wait, one of the guards shot at you?" Kennedy asked. "Kind of gives a certain impression, doesn't it?"

"Yeah, kinda threw up a red flag for me, so I'm looking into it," Edwards said. "At the very least, I can skulk around, maybe find an 'idiot's guide to operations'. You know, 'this is who we are and what we're up to' kind of thing."

"Yeah, sure, dude." Kennedy laughed. "How about we just get the hell out of here, hook up with the rest of our stick, and go home?"

The look on Edwards' face said it better than words could. "They're all dead."

"How?" asked Kennedy.

"Executed. All of them. Single gunshot to the back of the head, hands tied." Edwards sighed. "All very clinical. The same guards that shot at me and beat the hell out of you."

Kennedy punched the wall next to him and shook his head. He flexed his hands several times and paced around the room, swearing under his breath.

"It was a Sasquatch," Stacey said indignantly. "The same thing that killed my fiancé...er, my boyfriend."

"You two go, get to the surface, call the cops, the firehouse, anyone else that will answer the phone," Edwards said. "I'll poke around for a bit, then I'll join you on the surface."

"No way in hell," Kennedy said. "We need to stick together and figure this all out."

"No way," Edwards said. "That isn't going to happen. You guys won't be in harm's way because of me."

Edwards stood and walked across the room. He checked the coffeepot and looked for filters and coffee to make a pot. He gave up after a couple of minutes and settled on a cup of water.

"We could talk to the girls who run the office," Stacey said cheerily.

"What?" Kennedy asked. He turned his attention to where Stacey was sitting on the sofa against the door.

"Well, the way I see it, the girls who do the menial office tasks tend to have their fingers on the pulse of any given business," Stacey explained. "None of the documents are hidden or withheld. They can't be."

"Okay," Edwards relented. "We'll see if we can find some office help, find out why this outfit has a security branch that are such zealots. Once we determine that, we'll bug out. Maybe call the authorities once we get topside."

"Stace, did you see anything at the desk you were parked at a minute ago?" Kennedy asked.

"Like what?"

"Like a Rolodex or a phone roster?" Kennedy asked. "Maybe we can reach out and touch somebody!"

***

"Holly Andrews," she said into the phone receiver. She listened for several moments. "Yes, I can look into it," she said and set the receiver into the cradle. She sent a text message on her personal cell phone to a contact listed as "D". She stood, walked across the office, and clicked the door lock. She fished the cell phone out of her shirt and checked the display, then slid it back into place and walked back to her desk.

Clicking her way through the company Intranet, she soon found the icon for security footage and clicked on it. A prompt for a password popped up on the screen and she keyed it in—a jumble of numbers and alternatingly capitalized letters. It took her less than a minute to find the archived tape from the various cameras.

After browsing through dozens of thumbnails, most showing labs, mine tunnels, high traffic areas, and other strategic locations, she chose one to view. She watched several seconds of Vol-Corp, and witnessed Stacey being dragged into the holding cell. "She's kinda cute," she muttered.

Clicking on another icon, she watched a familiar face stare at her from the screen. She could not place a name to the face and stared at the screen. As she watched, the man, clad in a firefighter's coat and gear, walked obliviously past the camera. A second camera clip showed him cautiously approaching a security guard, who pulled a gun on him.

Holly smiled as the man tackled the guard and took the gun. The clip dropped out of the bottom of the handgrip, and he pulled the slide back. He tossed the empty gun one direction into the woods and the clip in the other.

"Who the hell are you?" she muttered, watching as he cuffed the man and carried him into the guard shack. "And why did they save this footage?"

She clicked through several more icons and watched quite a few more clips of security footage. Each time she saw the mystery man on the screen, she hoped even more that he would succeed.

***

Stacey dropped the receiver onto the cradle. "One of you guys can have a turn."

"How far did you get?" asked Kennedy.

"Twenty-five, no one answered," Stacey said, "but it's also super late. I think I am going to grab a quick nap on the couch." She yawned, and walked over to the sofa. "Wake me if you have any luck, okay, guys?"

"Yeah, I'll let you know," Kennedy said without looking up. He studied the list, and Edwards walked over.

"Any familiar names on the list?" Edwards asked. "A friend would be handy right about now."

"No," Kennedy said scanning the list. "Whoa, wait. Yeah. Do you remember Holly?"

"Holly? Holly McGrath? Navarro?" Edwards asked.

"No, Andrews."

"Really? Of course I do. You spent half of junior year pining over her," Edwards said and laughed. "If I recall, she dumped you for Deena Jackson."

"That's her," Kennedy said wistfully. "You never forget the one who gets away."

"Dude, if I remember, quite a few got away from you."

Kennedy shook his head and looked away. He slid open the drawer of the desk and grabbed a pen. He circled Holly's name and number on the phone sheet and propped his feet up on the desk. He leaned back in the chair.

"Really, smart-ass, name three," he demanded.

"First names, last names, or both first and last names?"

"Sure."

Edwards craned his neck in both directions, eliciting a pop on either side. "Let's see, there was McKenzie Shay, Katie McNamara, Alyson Reynolds, Tara Klein, Jessica—"

"Okay, okay, I get it," Kennedy said with a chuckle. "I dated a lot of girls in high school."

"That was freshman year." Edwards laughed. "You dated every girl in our class and probably bedded at least half!"

Kennedy shook his head and smiled. "I guess I did have a track record. So anyway, back on subject, I'm going to skip a few on the list, chief. I'm going to ring Holly, see what she's up to these days." He dialed the extension and waited.

"Holly Andrews," a familiar voice answered.

"Holly, this is Jason Kennedy. We briefly dated in high school, hopefully you remember me. I could use your help," Kennedy said evenly.

"Jason Kennedy, it has been over ten years...what kind of trouble are you in that you're calling me?" she asked. "Bail money?"

"Well, hell, Holly, where do I start?" Kennedy muttered. "For one, my entire hotshot crew is dead, I'm pretty much blind in my left eye from a

Sasquatch beating, and I've been told there is an army of psychotic security guys hunting for me. Oh, and I'm in a secret underground facility hidden in the middle of a nature preserve."

Edwards walked over to the desk and tapped the button for the speakerphone.

"Holly, this is Mike Edwards, I have a question for you. What does this outfit do?"

"Mike that is a long answer, and definitely not a phone conversation," Holly said. "Where are you guys, can you come to my office?"

"If I knew where we were, I'd gladly tell you," Edwards said.

"We can work our way to your office," Kennedy added.

"Okay, I'll be here, guys," she said. "My living quarters are attached to my office, and I have a private shower. We can discuss a few things."

"Okay, thank you, Holly, we'll be there as soon as we can," Kennedy said, hanging up the phone.

Edwards rooted through drawers and finally came up with a facility map. He laid it out on the desk and traced out a basic route. He and Kennedy discussed options. Holly's office was off the central corridor, four floors below their current location.

"I think since you have that fancy-assed guard coat, you should sneak around, maybe find a disguise for me and Stace," Kennedy said. "Like maybe some janitor's uniforms."

"You're an idiot," Edwards muttered. "We

should just wing it."

"Just go and find a janitor's closet. Maybe bring a mop bucket too."

"Fine, I'll see what I can do."

Edwards opened the door, and peaked out into the hallway. He saw a couple of people moving through the halls, most with files and coffee cups. He stepped out and clicked the door shut.

He glanced at his watch absently, then remembered it was broken. He walked through the hall, avoiding eye contact with anyone. He glanced at the signs for the doors, hoping to find the janitor's closet for this floor, before anyone stopped him.

"Excuse me," a voice said from behind him. "Hey, security guy, a little help?"

Edwards turned and looked at a short woman with a stack of files filling her arms, a dark brown purse hanging off a wrist, a coffee cup in her left hand, and an enormous set of keys dangling off the middle finger of her right hand.

"Thanks, big guy," she said, "Take my keys and unlock my door."

Edwards took her keys and began searching for an actual key. For each key on the ring, there were at least three keychain charms attached. He found the correct key and opened the door. He reached inside and flipped the light on for her.

"Thanks," she said. "Someone took the last file cart. That is always my luck!"

"You're welcome," Edwards said. "Do you know where the janitor's closet is?"

"Why, did you spill your coffee? Sorry, yeah, it's around the corner, three doors on the left."

"Is it locked?"

"Of course," she said and noticed the look in Edwards' eyes.

"My name is Victoria," she said as she looked through her keys. "Damn, hang on"—she walked over to the comically cluttered desk—"but everyone calls me Vic." She dug through the desk drawer and came up with a nearly empty key ring. She paused to brush a wisp of curly red hair out of her face. She presented the keys to him, holding it by a long key with a *J* engraved on it.

"Thanks," Edwards said. "Back in a minute." He walked to the closet and unlocked the door. He flicked the light on and entered. He looked around and stuffed two gray jumpsuits into an empty mop bucket. He stuffed the mop into it and shoved it out the door, pushing it with the mop handle. Edwards hustled back to Vic's office and dropped the keys off to her. He thanked her again and returned to the office where the three of them had hidden.

Edwards opened the door and stepped inside.

"Oh, thank God!" a woman crowed. "Security, these two weirdos were hiding in my office when I got here this morning. Get them out of here!"

"Yes, ma'am," Edwards answered. "Damned cleaning staff think they own the place!"

"Wait, Erica and Johann are gone?" the woman asked.

"Come on, you two," Edwards shouted, ignoring the woman. All three hustled out the door before the woman could ask any more questions.

CHAPTER TWELVE

"So let me get this straight," Holly said. "You clowns came out here to investigate a possible wildfire?"

"That's right," Kennedy said grandly. "It is what we do, you know, wildland firefighters? Smoke jumpers?"

"Our plane crashed," Edwards elaborated. "I was thrown out the door, and Jason rode it down. I'm guessing he was thrown out as well because he survived."

"The crash?" Holly asked, sipping an iced mocha. She had her feet propped up on her desk, a worn pair of slippers on her feet.

"No, the security around here," Edwards said. "I ended up hiking about a mile or so, found the guys in my outfit executed, and Jason missing. I got attacked by a goon with a gun and found a hidden facility in the woods. Overall, I'd say it's been a pretty busy day."

"You see, when the guards tossed the plane, they found seven duffel bags in the back and only five people in the fuselage," Kennedy explained. "So they called in their hunter team, which included a Sasquatch. It sure as hell didn't take long for that smelly bastard to find me. Worked me over pretty good too."

Holly sat silent for close to a minute, leaning on her elbows on the desk and pinching the bridge of her nose. She sighed and placed her palms flat on the desk. She looked from one man to the other.

"Probably one of the many unethical nano protocol tests," she said. "There is a lot of unethical, immoral, and flat-out illegal acts around here. In fact, this mining operation is operating illegally inside a federally sanctioned nature preserve."

Kennedy walked across the office like a caged animal, balling his hands into fists and relaxing them as he paced. Edwards sat in a leather chair off to the side of Holly's office as if it were a throne and he a king of old. The sound of a shower running in the other room created a low droning background noise.

"So this is a mining outfit?" demanded Kennedy. "What the hell kind of mining outfit does nano-machine testing on a Sasquatch? What kind of mining outfit kills people who get near their facility?"

"H.C. Wiln Company dabbles in technology, pharmaceuticals, nano-machinery, ore processing, oil, and just about any other lucrative venture they can buy out or blackmail into, not just mining," Holly said. "Trust me, I'm their corporate lawyer."

"How much of this 'dabbling' is done off the books?" asked Edwards.

"Most of it," she admitted. Holly unlocked a file drawer on her desk and retrieved a folder. She slid it across the surface toward Edwards. "They have a lot of straw companies and paper corporations. They own several of their own suppliers and at least one of their major competitors. The way it's going, they will have a monopoly within five years."

Edwards reached over and scooped up the file. He opened it and glanced through it. His eyes darted back and forth across the page, and he leaned forward slightly. He flipped to the next page.

"Son of a bitch," he muttered. "So what, you're a whistle-blower?"

She wrote a couple of lines on a Post-it note and handed it to him. The words "Not Here" were scrawled across it. He looked at her and handed the file to Kennedy, who began to read through it.

When he had finished reading the file, she placed it back into the drawer. She produced a black wallet and passed it to Edwards and Kennedy.

"That explains the file, then," Kennedy blurted.

"Hoo-ah," agreed Edwards.

"So, getting back on track, where does the chick figure into this?" Holly asked. "She doesn't strike me as a testosterone-driven, badass wildfire jock. Too girly." She shook her head, a tight grin on her face.

"I found her." Kennedy grinned. "I was 'volunteered'. When I woke up, there she was like a terrified angel."

"I see," Holly said. "So where do you go from here?"

Edwards sat silent for a moment, and Kennedy cleared his throat, glancing from one face to the next.

"I'm guessing they need to be stopped," Kennedy said. "I suppose that's what we'll do, citizen's-arrest the boss and get the hell out of here."

"Yeah, we can do that," Edwards said, a twinkle in his eye. The droning in the background went silent. Two minutes later, the door creaked open and Stacey walked into the office, toweling her hair dry. She sat down on the sofa at the edge of the office area and focused on getting her long brown hair dried. Kennedy walked to the bathroom and shut the door behind him.

"You're Wiln's corporate lawyer, does that include patents or contracts?" Edwards asked.

"Not really. At least I've never had to do anything with them, but I can do some digging. Contracts are easy. Why?" Holly said.

"Military contracts, specifically, nano-enhancements, mind control, that sort of thing," Edwards said. "There has to be a good reason for the goon squad. If I was developing those things, I'd definitely want to guard it. Maybe just some locked doors or a fence, but what the hell do I know."

"That shouldn't take too long, probably an hour or so," Holly said as she checked her cell phone while typing on the laptop on her desk.

"So, Mike, what'd I miss?" blurted Stacey, her spirit buoyed by the shower.

"Not much," lied Edwards. "Holly, Jason, and I went to high school together."

"I see," she muttered. "So what, just catching up on old times?"

"You could say that," Edwards muttered.

***

Edwards was up and making coffee less than three hours after he finished showering. He had slept on the floor of the office, next to the door.

He sat at Holly's desk, sipping a steaming mug of coffee and contemplating his plan as Holly stepped out into the office space. She walked straight to the coffeepot, poured herself a cup, and spooned in creamer and sugar.

"Morning," she muttered. "Did you sleep at all?"

"Oh, yeah," Edwards said. "More than enough."

"I looked into Wiln's military contracts, and they are working on quite a few innovations. Nano-enhancements, integrated HUD's, self-replicating body armor, controlled-burst electromagnetic pulse, and nano-medic technology. With the right research and funding, this quite possibly may launch humanity into a kind of immortality. They're at least ten years ahead of their closest competitor," she said. "Possibly more like twenty."

"What are they doing in the civilian sector?"

"Tens of millions of dollars, at the very least," she said. "And they do not have permission to operate this facility, nor did they go through the proper channels for any of the testing."

"I'd say that's enough for the security detail," Edwards muttered. "But having those guys prepped to kill?"

"I may have an answer for that," Kennedy offered. "Do you remember the rumors, Mike?"

"The ones about heavy metal poisoning and other suspicious circumstances?"

"That's it," Kennedy answered. "It just so happens those particular chemicals are used in processing ore into gold."

"Gold, eh," remarked Edwards. "You don't say…"

"I certainly do," Kennedy continued. "My theory, if you will—they're up here mining for coal, illegally I might add, and they find gold or maybe platinum, or who in God's name knows or cares, for that matter. Anyway, they find the stuff, and that pays the way for the technology advances and nano-research. Money talks, and bada-bing, they're well on their way to being the top tech provider to Uncle Sam!"

Edwards sat for a moment, finger tapping against his chin. "Makes sense, but where do we go from here?"

"Here, Mike," Holly said, holding out a flash drive. "This is all the research files on all three phases of the nano-tech R and D."

"Three phases?" asked Kennedy.

"Body, mind, and spirit," Holly answered. "I forwarded the information about the unethical testing to my office in an encrypted e-mail."

"I've got *body*," quipped Kennedy. "And I've experienced *mind* firsthand, but what the hell does *spirit* have to do with it?"

"Not sure," Holly admitted. "I've already informed my superiors of your arrival, and I've been ordered to bug out. Soon. I've been given twelve hours. They seem to think you guys will bumble around and get captured, tortured, and turn on me to save yourselves."

Edwards and Kennedy both laughed.

"They don't know us very well, do they, Jason?" Edwards said. "Here's my thought: Go now. The three of us will do the dirty work and drag the boss out to you and your people. Kicking and screaming, if necessary. Actually, based on what I've witnessed so far, maybe kicking and screaming is preferable. Might give us a little leverage."

"Sounds like a plan," Kennedy said. "One thing, though, we don't even know the dude's name, let alone where he is."

"Willem Mancirotti," offered Holly as she handed them a map of the facility. "I circled his office on the map."

"So I have to ask," Kennedy said. "What do we do with this information?"

"Holly shrugged, raising her hands. "Do what you think is right. Just remember how you got it, okay?"

"Jason, go wake Stacey," Edwards said. "Holly, get your coat. It's time for you to pack. Jason, we got some planning to do."

CHAPTER THIRTEEN

Kennedy, Stacey, and Edwards left Holly's office, bidding the corporate lawyer good luck. Holly had her name tag clipped to her shirt and a large floral print beach tote tucked under her arm. It had taken some doing, but she had arranged to take a week of vacation time.

The smoke jumpers and Stacey walked around the corner and toward the elevator. Moving slowly, they silently crossed the hallway.

"According to this, Mancirotti's office is in the center of the central column, at the very top," Edwards said. "Just below the surface. If luck is on our side, there will be a side exit." The map was tucked safely into a pocket on his vest.

The elevator doors opened with a ding, and the three of them stepped inside. Once the doors shut, Edwards produced a set of universal elevator door keys and locked the doors. He pulled the map out and opened it. He studied it intently.

"Okay, so Holly's office is fourth level down at the outside edge of the facility," Edwards said. "We need to make our way through Mine Maintenance to an area labeled Town. After that, it's a half mile to central shaft."

"This place is huge," Kennedy said. "It's at least a mile to the far end of Mine Maintenance."

"Yeah, so?" Edwards asked, half listening. Stacey looked on, her faith firmly planted in two men she had just met.

"There's at least four security checkpoints, and whatever 'town' actually is," Kennedy replied. "And on top of that, my ankle sucks, and we need to keep Stacy safe. Now, how do we accomplish all of that with only a pair of brass knuckles and a couple of Ka-bars?"

"I have a plan," Edwards said boldly. "Well, not really a plan, per se, but an idea of what we can do."

"Nice," Kennedy muttered. "Maybe at some point we can put our heads together and make the idea you have into a workable half-assed scheme."

"Uh, guys," Stacey said quietly, "I can help out. I am not helpless, you know."

Both men looked at her at the same time, a somewhat embarrassed look on their faces. They quickly returned their attention to the map.

"Of course," Edwards said awkwardly. "No one said you were helpless. Jason and I both have been in combat and have had training to survive just about any situation."

"Yeah, and because I'm a woman you think I can't take care of myself?"

"No, but there are hundreds of men with guns, with orders to kill us on sight," Kennedy said. "And we have been shot at before. I was over in Afghanistan, and when an IED blew up the lead vehicle of the last patrol I was on, a bit of shrapnel embedded itself in my shoulder. The docs said that I was unfit for service."

"I never knew you were in the military," Stacey said. "You never told me that. I have two big strong veterans watching out for me!"

A smirk was all Edwards offered, and Kennedy sighed.

"I was never military," he said. "I was a civilian operator."

"What's that even mean?" Stacey asked and looked at the elevator doors.

"Basically, I was a civilian soldier, a mercenary," Kennedy explained. "I joined the army infantry. I was half through basic when I cold-cocked my senior drill instructor. Knocked his ass out cold with one punch."

"Really?" she asked. "Kind of seeing a pattern, Jason."

"Yeah." He smiled. "Anyway, dude was a pinhead, and I got kicked out. Went over anyway as an operator."

"Alright," Edwards said and shook his head.

"Let's go."

He turned the key and reactivated the elevator doors, and then pushed the button to open them. They stepped out of the elevator cab and walked down the hallway, a long stretch of painted rock with crude overhead lighting and the occasional doorway chiseled out of the stone.

They walked in the center of the hallway until they heard a long whirring noise reverberating off the hard walls of the corridor.

"What the hell is that?" asked Stacey.

"Sounds like a golf cart," Kennedy said.

Looking around, Edwards sidestepped over to a doorway and tried the handle. "Come on," he whispered, hoping the door was unlocked. To his relief, the handle turned and the latch clicked open.

"Let's go!" he hissed through clenched teeth, as the sound of the cart grew closer. No sooner had they clicked the door shut behind them when the cart whizzed past, not even slowing a fraction.

Edwards rested his forehead against the wooden door, breathing slowly and steadily. A cough behind him alerted him to a presence in the room with them.

"Uh, excuse me?" a meek voice said. "Who are you?"

Edwards whipped his head around and saw a short man with thick glasses and short, cut hair. He wore a rumpled black suit and brown loafers.

"Name is Langstrom," Edwards lied. "Security.

I'm taking these two on a tour of the facility. They're thinking of transferring to security detail."

"Oh, that's nice," the man said. "My name is Mitchell, I'm part of product sales."

"Excellent," Edwards said quickly. "Carry on, then."

Edwards threw the door open, peered out, and not seeing the cart or any other living soul in the hall, bound through it. He jogged at a pace he knew Kennedy and Stacey would be able to match. They ran, looking at the doors, dotting the walls at sporadic intervals. After what seemed like an hour, they reached the end of the long, twisting hallway.

The walls and floor were rougher than at the beginning of the hall, the stone of the mine was visible, and there was no attempt at creature comforts. Incandescent bulbs in gray steel cages cast a sickly yellow glow at sporadic intervals. In the dim light, they were able to make out the details of the hallway.

A sign depicting a hard hat and safety goggles was plastered to the walls, and caution signs lined the wall to their left. A small rack on the wall held prepackaged personal protective gear for visitors.

"This must be it," Kennedy said grandly. "Last stop, Bedrock."

Stacey was leaning against the wall catching her breath. Kennedy was breathing normally but wincing each time he put weight on his left foot.

"Your ankle okay?" asked Edwards.

"Yeah," he said. "I'll be fine." He stooped over and tied the laces tighter.

Edwards reached out and opened the door. Inside was a large cavern with various equipment in different states of disrepair sitting in rough-cut niches in the stone walls. The ceiling was well over thirty feet high.

The group froze for a moment, hearing a buzzing noise off to one side of them. They silently crept to the nearest niche and ducked behind some wooden shipping crates. The opening was twenty feet long and nearly as deep, with crates just inside the arched doorway.

Kennedy searched, turning slowly until he found the source of the noise.

"Two guys, about fifty yards to our right," Kennedy whispered. "Looks like they're building a hopper. The noise is the welder."

"Okay, so what, we go straight up the middle, then?" asked Edwards.

"Works for me," Kennedy muttered.

"Uh, guys?" Stacey said softly. "What's a hopper?" She was looking at the main path running through the center of the maintenance cavern. There was a look of concern on her pretty face.

"It's kind of like a big steel funnel," Edwards murmured. He was looking around as well and straining to see if there was anyone else moving around. "It drops material onto conveyor belts."

"Okay, we have other problems, then," Stacey

whispered. She pointed. "Two guys in a golf cart thing, with guns. And they are coming this way."

"Shit," said Kennedy. "Okay, no worries, we can handle this."

Stacey felt a sense of panic welling up, and as she looked from one man to the other, she saw that Kennedy was a shining example of calm and Edwards was in thought, a calm look on his face as well. He raised a hand up and glanced at the cuticles of his first and second fingers.

The sound of tires crunching over loose gravel drew closer, then stopped. The headlights of the small electric vehicle shone brightly on the crates, and then swung away, angling further down the tunnel. A small, hand-operated searchlight clicked on, bathing the area in dazzling white light. The light stopped on the crate Stacey and the firefighters were hiding behind.

"Stop," one of the men riding in the cart said. "Hold up a sec, Ed. I think I see something." The cart stopped, and the guard stepped out with a grunt. A flashlight clicked on, and the guard walked to the edge of the crates. He looked around, swinging the flashlight closer to where Stacey, Kennedy, and Edwards were hiding.

"What is it?" demanded Ed, the guard at the wheel.

"Nothin'," the man said. He was starting to turn when Kennedy sprang to his feet, hooking a brawny arm around the guard's throat. He pulled the man over the crate backward.

Edwards threw a solid knockout punch, catching the man square in the temple.

The flashlight, a heavy aluminum model holding three D-cell batteries, slipped from the now unconscious guard's grip. Both men saw the Mag-light fall.

Stacey calmly caught the light seconds before it hit the hard stone floor. She clicked it off and set it down on the floor next to her without a sound. She looked up, glancing from one man to the other.

"Nice," Kennedy mouthed. Stacey grinned back at him.

"Hey!" the other guard yelled. "Where the hell did you get off to? Jim, you asshole! You better not be sneaking a smoke without me!"

The sound of the guard exiting the golf cart was followed by boots on stone as the guard made his way to the crates trying to see a burning cigarette, Jim's flashlight, or both.

"Jim," the guard called, listening for a response. He waited half a minute, then removed the flashlight from his belt, clicked the light on, and shone it around. When he circled it back around, he stood looking face to face with Edwards.

"Hi," Edwards said cheerily, grinning like an idiot. He lashed out and landed a viscous uppercut on the guard's chin, nearly lifting him off his feet. As the man backpedaled, Edwards shot a hard jab landing directly between his eyes. He crumpled to the floor unconscious.

"You do nice work!" Kennedy remarked. He searched both guards' pockets and came up with two partial packs of cigarettes. "Score!"

"Why, thank you," Edwards shot back. "So nice of you to notice!"

"I couldn't help but notice," Kennedy said. He tucked the cigarettes into his pockets. "It's been ages since I witnessed work this nice."

"I try," Edwards smugly said.

"It shows," countered Kennedy.

"Guys!" Stacey shouted. "Enough! We gotta go. You can admire one another later."

"You heard the lady, Jason," Edwards said, picking up where he left off. "After you."

"No, after you," Kennedy said.

"I insist!" Edwards offered.

"Come on!" Stacey said, rolling her eyes. She grabbed their arms and half dragged them behind her.

CHAPTER FOURTEEN

The phone trilled. A large hand shot from the top of the desk. "Security, Gonzales," a voice said. A long pause while the caller spoke, and then, "Yes sir, I'll take care of it."

He turned toward the monitor on the large, nearly empty steel desk top. He clicked through several files on the desktop image on the computer and pulled up pictures of two men. The men were clad in Nomex. One was unconscious and the other was in the woods above the facility, held at gunpoint by one of the security guards. The man in the woods was in a short video clip. The clip showed the guard pulling a gun and the man disarming him and tossing the gun into the woods.

He flipped through several more files and watched several clips of security camera footage. He saw the other man and a woman exiting the volunteer holding cell and entering the storeroom across the hall.

He picked up the phone on his desk and dialed a number.

"Central security," the voice said. "This is George."

"This is Gonzales," the head of security said. "Where are those three people now?"

"The last time they were seen, they were entering Mine Maintenance," George said.

"Double the guard presence in the mine. I want these people found immediately," Gonzales said, rubbing a meaty hand on his forehead.

"Yes, sir," George said. "I'll make it happen."

Gonzales dropped the phone back onto the cradle and laced his fingers behind his head. He sighed deeply and closed his eyes for a moment. He opened his eyes, picked up the receiver, and dialed a number.

"Mancirotti," a crisp baritone answered.

"Mister Mancirotti," Gonzales started timidly. "This is Gonzales. We traced the firemen to Mine Maintenance. We are doubling our presence in the mine."

"Understood. Do what it takes," Mancirotti replied, careful to avoid any incriminating statement. "How is everything topside?"

"Cleanup is finished," Gonzales said.

"Good. Clean up the last two and any other loose ends," Mancirotti said and hung up the phone.

Gonzales rubbed his temples, a headache

starting to develop. He leaned back in his chair, stared at the ceiling, and sighed.

Chapter Fifteen

Edwards stared toward the open hallway and listened as Kennedy and Stacey slept. They were holed up in a small alcove just off the main tunnel. He sighed and stretched. After he had repositioned, he reached into a pocket and fished out the flash drive Holly had given him.

Turning it over in his hand, he stared at it for several minutes. His thoughts strayed, imagining the possibilities.

"What do you have there, Mikey?"

"What? Nothing," he said, distracted. He slipped the flash drive back into his pocket. "Is it time for me to sack out?"

"Nah, I couldn't sleep," Kennedy said, lighting a cigarette. He took a deep drag off it, hidden in his hand. He exhaled and offered it to Edwards, who took it. Edwards took a drag and passed it back.

"You need to sleep, dude," Edwards said. "It has been one hell of a long day."

"Yeah, I know," Kennedy said weakly. "There's one thing that has been buggin' me — the flash drive with all the research notes."

"What about it?" Edwards asked.

"What are we doing with it?"

"Not sure," Edwards said. "The way I see it, it is one hell of an ethical quandary. On the one hand, we could keep it to ourselves and start a multimillion dollar business just by selling off one percent of it. On the other hand, we should give it to the authorities to sort out."

"Yeah, that's how I see it too," Kennedy said. "If it's all the same, I think we should keep it and never have to work again. We could be billionaires. If this outfit is half of what Holly says, then Abbey's grandkids will never have to work."

Edwards stood and walked from one end of the room to the next and sighed. He was getting restless and anxious to get on with the task at hand.

"I'm going to lay down for a few minutes, come get me when..." Kennedy trailed off.

A footfall, followed by a cough, alerted the men. Looking down the hall, a security guard stood silhouetted in the doorway at the end of the corridor. He started a slow, meandering saunter down the hallway.

Kennedy and Edwards melted back into the shadows of the alcove. A quick glance over his shoulder told Kennedy that Stacey was still asleep. A simple glance between them solidified their course of action.

The minutes seemed to stretch into hours as the security guard sauntered down the hallway, first looking into an alcove on one side, then the other. He did not appear to be in any kind of hurry. His revolver was held in his right hand, in a lazy ready position near his shoulder. He held a flashlight out in front of his body, lighting his path.

Edwards slowed his breathing and slid the brass knuckles out of his pocket. Kennedy gently clamped a hand over Stacey's mouth, waking her up. She sat silently and watched as Kennedy pressed a finger against his lips, then pointed. She nodded. Her eyes were wide, but she calmed down a moment later.

The guard stopped at the opening of the alcove and shone his flashlight to the back of the small space. As he was swinging toward the right side opening, Kennedy reached out and grabbed the guard's right arm and yanked him into the stone doorway.

No sooner had the man's face slammed into the stone, Edwards' brass-knuckled fist slammed into the side of his head. The guard crumpled to the ground in an unconscious heap. A shot echoed throughout the cavernous space.

"What the hell?" Kennedy breathed.

"That one had a friend, Jason," Edwards whispered as he peered out past the archway.

Kennedy scooped up the fallen revolver and

held it out toward the source of the shot. He squeezed off a shot, then withdrew his arm. Two more shots rang out, and Kennedy answered with one of his own. He had a fix on the shooter.

"Mike, he should only have three shots left, then he'll have to reload," Kennedy said.

"Central security command, do you copy?" The radio on the unconscious guard's belt crackled to life.

Edwards practically dove across the alcove opening and scrambled to grab the radio. As he was picking it up, it crackled again.

"This is central, go ahead."

"Central, this is—" was all that Edwards heard before he keyed the mic button. Edwards held his breath, hoping that his radio walked over the other transmission on the frequency. He held it until he heard the sound of open line.

"Say again," the voice from central command said. "Say again, last."

"Central, I've—" Edwards again interrupted the conversation.

The security guard fired another two shots, and Kennedy lobbed one back at him, continuing the standoff.

"One left," Kennedy said. "It's pretty much *go-time*, Mikey!"

"Stacey!" Edwards said in a harsh whisper. She crossed the alcove and stopped by his side. "Here, as soon as that goon out there starts talking, hold this button down. Hold it until the son of a bitch stops talking."

She took the radio and nodded. "Okay," she said. Her eyes were wide with fear, and she was nearly shaking.

"I'll be right back," Edwards said. He ducked around the edge of the alcove opening as Kennedy was sticking his hand into the opening. He fired a shot, and as he withdrew, the guard fired his return shot. The bullet grazed the back of Kennedy's hand.

"Dammit," he groaned but held onto the revolver. "Go, Mike. He should be reloading right now!"

Edwards rolled out away from the alcove and popped to his feet in a full sprint. He ran as fast as he possibly could and saw the guard ducked down behind a golf cart.

As he approached, the guard was just raising up and had fired when he spotted Edwards. The security guard swiveled, drew a quick bead on the smoke jumper, and pulled the trigger.

Edwards dropped into a baseball slide, feet first, and came to a stop alongside the front of the golf cart as the weapon offered nothing but a solid click.

Edwards bound across the gap, partially diving through the golf cart, and landed a solid punch on the side of the guard's head. The man reeled and Edwards followed up with a right hand which, with the brass knuckles still in place, succeeded in knocking the guard out.

Edwards worked quickly and soon had the guard cuffed. The chain on the cuffs run underneath his belt and clicked around his left arm and right ankle. He scooped up the guard's weapon and whistled, three short notes followed by one long note.

Kennedy stepped out into the cavern and walked toward the spot Edwards stood. He dropped the now-empty revolver on the cavern floor.

"Oh, shit," he muttered when Edwards held up the Colt model 1911. "I thought all these guys had revolvers."

"Guess not," Edwards said as he offered the weapon to Kennedy, hand grip first. "Thing jammed on him, otherwise this little circus would be one clown short."

"You have all the luck," Kennedy said. "I've always been stuck with dashing good looks, a silver tongue, this amazing body, and I am most definitely the brains of this outfit. You always have been the one with all the luck."

"Well, mister 'brains of this outfit', you're bleeding like a stuck pig," Stacey said pointing. "May want to take care of that."

Kennedy looked down and saw the groove the bullet traced across the back of his hand. "So I am," he said. "That must be why we keep you around."

"This is central," the radio crackled, interrupting the conversation. "Return your handset, swap it out for a fresh one. Yours must be broken."

Edwards reached out and grabbed the radio in Stacey's hand, keying the mic. "Roger," he shouted.

Kennedy visibly winced and waited for a response or a demand for identification. When a full minute had passed and nothing happened, he chuckled.

"Let's go, guys," Stacey said.

"No point in sticking around here," Kennedy said. "Our friends don't want to play anymore."

"It's a good thing there are dozens more here," Edwards said. "I bet we'll find some more friends soon enough."

CHAPTER SIXTEEN

The small electric cart zipped through the wide stone tunnels with little more than a droning whir.

"We can't keep it, you know," Edwards said from behind the wheel. "There is probably some way for the goons to track these things."

"Yeah," Kennedy said. "But that doesn't mean we have to hoof it for this whole silly field trip. I say we ride and glide for a while. Save on the walking as long as we can."

The radio crackled, and the sound of central security talking to a pair of guards somewhere in the mine was heard. A response came, and then silence again.

"Good call taking the radio," Kennedy said, leaning back to talk to Stacey.

All three of them were wearing security jackets, and Stacey's long hair was tucked up under a black baseball cap. The security jacket she wore was comically too big for her. It made her look like a little girl wearing her father's clothes.

They passed another security cart going in the opposite direction. The men waved as Stacey pantomimed sneezing. As soon as they had passed by, Stacey turned and watched as their taillights disappeared into the distance. Stacey exhaled the breath she had been holding in a big sigh.

"This is freaking me out," she said. "The sooner we're out of here, the better."

They drove in silence for over a minute until they found an empty alcove and pulled the cart into it. Edwards pulled the map out of his pocket and unfolded it. Kennedy propped his feet up on the front cowl of the cart. He lit a cigarette and took a dramatic drag on it. He held the cigarette in his mouth and leaned his head back, nearly into the jump seat bolted in the rear. Stacey playfully pushed his head back upright.

"We're here," he muttered, studying the map. "We should be coming to the edge of maintenance soon. Once we get there, it'll be a short trip through 'town', then onto central shaft."

"Oh good," Kennedy sneered, ashing on the mine floor. "I was worried our little walking vacation would end too soon. How far to town?"

"Should be within ten minutes," Edwards said offhandedly, "Then town, not sure what we'll find there."

Stacey was watching behind them nervously. "Okay, let's keep moving."

The cart pulled forward a couple of feet and swung wide to the right. Edwards turned the key, putting the electric vehicle into reverse. A beeping noise echoed in the alcove. It seemed deafening to them, and Edwards flipped the key to its neutral detent.

"Damn, that seems pretty loud, doesn't it," he chuckled. He put it back into reverse and floored it, causing the back tires to spin ineffectively on the loose gravel on the alcove floor.

Edwards backed off the accelerator, allowing the tires to catch some traction, pushing the small cart backward until they were clear of the alcove. Switching the key again, they set off, passing alcoves and the occasional doorway. When the doorways started to appear closer together, Edwards swung the vehicle in a wide arc and stopped it. He turned the key to the off position and sat back.

"We really need to lose the cart," Edwards said at length. "It'd arouse less suspicion if we were to lose the guard uniforms too."

"Yeah, you're prob'ly right," Kennedy muttered. He hopped out and offered his hand to Stacey. "Depending on what the hell *town* is, it may be better to hoof it in plain clothes."

"Thanks," she said softly, taking his hand and stepping out of the cart. She blushed as she realized she held his hand for much longer than she had anticipated. She felt a rush of heat and smiled.

Kennedy smiled and pulled his hand back. He lit a cigarette and tossed the empty pack into the golf cart. "Let's go."

"Wait, we don't want to leave this here, do we?" Edwards asked grinning. "Don't want to abandon it here, that would be rude."

"The right thing to do would be to return it," Kennedy said smiling.

"What are you guys doing?" asked Stacey. She was answered by both men grinning.

He reached into the IFAK on his belt and brought out a thick roll of medical tape. He wrapped the tape around the accelerator and looped it around the canopy support. He pressed the accelerator down and pulled it tight, keeping the pedal down. He added wraps until he was satisfied it would hold.

"Jason, would you give me a hand?" Edwards asked, walking to the back of the cart. Kennedy joined him, and as one they lifted the back of the cart off the ground several inches.

"Stacey, reach in and put it in forward," Edwards said. "Then clear out. Fast."

She reached inside and turned the key. The rear tires began to spin. She stepped out of the way and walked to the back of the cart. As soon as she was next to Kennedy, they dropped the back of the cart and watched as it careened off into the distance.

"Listen for that," Edwards said. "I'm sure our missing cart will create a sensation."

"We are doing the polite thing," Kennedy said smiling. "We're retuning it. Probably not the right way though. I guess there is more than one way to do things."

Stacey and the smoke jumpers set off, walking for what seemed like an hour before Edwards cleared his throat.

"Hey, Jason, what time you got?" he asked. He took the watch off his wrist and put it into the IFAK.

"Pushing five," Kennedy said offhandedly.

The doors had been spread out several hundred feet apart, and now they were becoming closer together. As they walked, the wide tunnel began to grow narrower, a little at first, then more and more noticeably. They had been walking for a while and barely noticed when the stone walls gave way to brick walls.

Soon, there was only glass storefront and neon signs as far as the eye could see. There was signs offering food and grocery items. Some offered tobacco products and beverages. All of them had neon signs and products in the windows.

Kennedy ducked into one and was back out a few minutes later. He jogged to catch up to Edwards and Stacey. He held a pack of cigarette in his hand, as well as a couple of bottles of water.

"Here," he said, holding out the bottles of water. "We really need to watch ourselves. There are security guys in every store. Good news, though, there's no need for cash. You can just sign for everything, and they deduct it from your pay."

"One thing, one minor little thing: you don't work here, dumbass!" Edwards quipped.

"It's okay, I signed your name anyway," Kennedy shot back.

"Oh, great! That's going to come out of my expense account!" Edwards announced. "You owe me for that! I scrimp and save, trying to stretch the budget for as long as possible."

"It's okay, we can stop for some food and you can sign my name for it, I suppose." Kennedy shrugged. "I'll never make budget this month anyway."

Stacey rolled her eyes and kept walking. She smirked and ignored the near-constant banter between the firefighters.

"So, where is a good place to eat here in town?" asked Kennedy.

"I hear good things about that place," Edwards said pointing. "They have great matzah balls."

"Nah," Kennedy smirked. "I hear they have soggy fish and skimpy cannoli."

"How about there?" Stacey asked pointing. "Can't go wrong with that. A burger and some fries sounds fantastic."

"I can't disagree. Hang out here," Edwards said. "I'll be right back. He walked across the street and ducked into the door. He ordered, then waited while the order was filled.

Once the meal was ready, and he was sitting at the counter, he signed for the food and walked quickly back to where he had left Kennedy and Stacey. He whistled three short whistles and one long one and waited. A moment later, Stacey and Kennedy exited a nearby shop and joined Edwards.

"We got some more bottled water and a few other things we can use," Stacey said with a smile.

"We can have a hot meal for now and figure out the next move later on," Kennedy said. "That will be the best thing for us right now, as far as I'm concerned."

Edwards tossed a bag of food toward Kennedy and handed another to Stacey. He sat down on a bench and opened his own bag. "It's just a burger and fries," he said. "Basic, but none of us have eaten in quite a while. Besides, anything would taste great at this point."

Stacey broke the silence after nearly two minutes. "Jason," she asked, "whatcha doing?"

"Hmm?" he said. "Just eating."

He continued to bunch fries together in stacks of nine, sorted by length, and ate them. There were several mismatched ones on the edge of the wrapper in front of him.

"He's got some OCD," Edwards muttered. "You should see when someone leaves cook time on the microwave at the firehouse! He goes bat-shit crazy!"

"Yeah, well, not all of us have military training

in eating fast," Kennedy shot back. "This guy used to eat everything in counts of three."

"I got over it." Edwards shrugged.

"You're both nuts," Stacey said and laughed. She stopped suddenly, all color draining from her face.

Edwards and Kennedy both saw her face at the same time and reacted, one man turning to look while the other stood and excused himself. Kennedy watched as a patrol of security guards strolled through town.

"Stace, breathe," Kennedy hissed through clenched teeth. "Breathe, or you're going to draw attention to us."

She continued to stare, but she took a deep breath and hissed it out through her teeth. Her breathing slowed a fraction. She was clearly rattled but she did as she was told.

"Stacey!" Kennedy barked, glancing toward the security patrol. He saw one of the guards starting to walk in their direction. Kennedy grabbed her shoulders and pulled her to him, kissing her. She stiffened, then relaxed. Her hand slid up his arm and wrapped around his neck.

Edwards had circled behind the guards and was following several paces behind. He saw one of the security men stare toward Kennedy and Stacey's position and began running scenarios through his head. He had decided on a course of action and just pulled the brass knuckles out of his pocket when Kennedy grabbed Stacey and kissed her. They were still kissing when the patrol passed, and Edwards came alongside them. He saw the guard staring at them shake his head and keep walking, ignoring them.

Edwards stood awkwardly, waiting for Kennedy or Stacey to break off the kiss. Finally, after a couple of minutes, he coughed loudly.

"Oh, hey Mike," Kennedy said while Stacey blushed. "I suppose the guards are gone?"

Chapter Seventeen

"We need to find a hiding place," Edwards said. "Somewhere to lay low for a while."

"Yeah," said Kennedy. "There's an alley not far from here — if it's there for trash cans only, it might work for us."

"Lead on then, my good man," Edwards said grinning.

"Let's just go," Stacey said, stopping the banter before it began. Kennedy looked around and pointed. He led the way, followed by Stacey, and then Edwards. As they were approaching the alley, a golf cart zipped past. Tires screeching on pavement echoed among the brick and glass of town.

"This may get interesting," Kennedy remarked.

Edwards ducked into a storefront and was right back out again in a moment. He was carrying a push broom over his shoulder. He winked at Kennedy and smiled reassuringly at Stacey. He whistled a familiar, yet unnamable tune while he unscrewed the head from the handle.

The cart wheeled around, tires screaming in protest. The men in the front seat sat, eyes locked on the three people standing in the middle of the street. The passenger drew his sidearm and held it at the ready.

Staring at the cart as it sped toward them, Edwards and Kennedy were calm. Stacey bolted, stepping inside a nearby storefront.

"Come on, then!" shouted Edwards. He threw the broom head as hard as he could. Coming to a stop directly in front of the cart's front tires, it caused the vehicle to lose control.

Both men climbed out of the golf cart and stood next to it. *"Freeze!"* the driver shouted. He drew his sidearm and aimed.

Edwards threw the broom handle like a spear, hitting the man's hand and knocking the gun from his grasp.

Kennedy pulled the Colt from his waistband and aimed. "Drop your gun," he called. The passenger stared at him a moment. He fired a shot, hitting the front tire of the cart. "I mean it!"

The passenger lowered his gun and held his hands up. Kennedy held his aim as Edwards walked toward the men.

"How you doing, guys," Edwards said boisterously. He pulled the cuffs off one man's belt and clicked it shut around his right wrist. The guard swung a quick left cross, catching Edwards hard on the chin. Kennedy sprinted over and grabbed the other guard in a headlock.

Rubbing his chin, Edwards looked at the guard. "I was going to be a nice guy about this." He swung a punch of his own. A resounding clang filled the street. The guard crumpled to the ground, unconscious. "Jason, needin' some help?"

"If you have a minute," Kennedy said, "I'd be thrilled to witness some more of your work!"

Edwards walked over, snapped the handcuffs onto the guard's wrists, and shoved him to the ground. "Time to go," he muttered. With Kennedy's help, he hoisted the man and dropped him into the back of the cart.

Kennedy dragged the other man into the cart and climbed into the driver's seat.

"Where you heading?" Edwards asked.

"Nowhere in particular," he answered. "Probably a few blocks over, and then a nice little out-of-the-way dumpster for these guys."

Stacey walked over, a smile on her face. She held out a roll of duct tape. "This will help keep them quiet for a while."

"Thank you, Stace," Kennedy said. "You're a peach." He took the tape and put a piece on both guards' mouths.

Edwards and Stacey waited while the cart pulled away. They waited a moment, then ducked into a storefront waiting for Kennedy to return.

"So, is Jason seeing anyone?"

Edwards laughed. "What? Are you interested?"

"No," she answered far too quickly. "Just making conversation." She looked away as she felt her cheeks growing hot. "I hardly know you two, and you're risking your lives for me. I just want to get to know the men who are getting me out of here."

"Sure," Edwards said. "Anyway, no, he isn't seeing anyone. For the record, I haven't seen him look at a woman the way he looks at you. For what that's worth. He always stays aloof, guarded. With you, it's more like adoration."

She smiled and continued to browse. She pulled a package off a hook and handed it to Edwards. He carried it with him and plucked a few more items off of shelves. He glanced out the window and saw no one on the street. They grabbed a few bottles of water and signed for them at the counter.

"You from maintenance?" the shop clerk asked.

"Yeah," Edwards said. "Name is Langstrom, and this is Candace. She's a trainee. Need to get her a basic tool set."

"Pretty late, isn't it?"

"First chance we've had," Edwards said. "Onboarding stuff, training videos, the whole nine yards."

"If there is anything else you need, just let me know," he said slipping everything into a plastic bag. "I can order just about anything."

Edwards and Stacey left the hardware store and walked across the street. Kennedy was sitting on a bench leaning back, feet crossed in front of him.

"Hey," he said, "get anything good?"

"A few wrenches and some water," Stacey said. "And I got a sweatshirt. It's cold in here!"

"What the hell do we need wrenches for?" he asked.

"I'm sure you guys can find a use for them. They're adjustable!" She smiled.

Edwards shrugged while Kennedy led the way to the alley he had spotted earlier. Edwards and Stacey stood outside while Kennedy walked into the alley. A moment later, three short whistles and one long one sounded from it.

"Ladies first," Edwards said. "This is home for the night."

CHAPTER EIGHTEEN

Edwards and Kennedy sat in the alley waiting out the night. They had been caught up in a debate and for the last twenty minutes had been full-on arguing.

Kennedy lit a cigarette, concealed it in his fist, and took drags off it occasionally.

"You're nuts," Kennedy said shaking his head. "Let's sell it all and skip the country!"

"I think we should oversee the research and make sure this," — Edwards gestured around them — "doesn't happen again. Besides, I'm sure that it'd stay legit if we continue the research and not just sell to the highest bidder. Can you imagine a terrorist group with this kind of sophisticated tech? Any country that hates America would kill for some of this stuff. Especially if it's like Holly described."

"Yeah," Kennedy said. "One problem. We don't know anything about this kind of work. I reckon we could look at it from an entrepreneurial stance. Hire some geeks to do the heavy lifting."

"You're talking quite a staff—scientists, engineers, and others," Edwards said thoughtfully. "I'm sure we can figure out how to offer competitive wages."

"We'll Google it," Kennedy said grinning. "How hard can it be?"

They sat in contemplative silence for several minutes. They watched as people walked past the alley. The number of people walking around town was steadily decreasing as the night wore on.

Stacey padded over to the spot where the men were sitting. She yawned silently, lifted a bottle of water, and sipped it.

"So what are we talking about?" she asked. "The research Holly gave us?"

"*Us?*" asked Kennedy.

"Yeah, us," she replied, hands on her hips. "I'm a part of this. If we make it out of here, I say we oversee the research and produce the nano-machines and everything. Split the whole thing three ways. Give Holly a fair share, of course, set her up for life."

"Why?" asked Edwards. "I don't disagree, but why?"

"If this information falls into the wrong hands, all of this stupidity will happen again," Stacey said. "We don't want any more assholes in charge of this kind of revolutionary technology. We're witnessing firsthand the results of greed. Besides that, this stuff belongs to the public. It will revolutionize the way we live!"

"This is a conversation for another day," Edwards interjected. Kennedy was sitting silent, studying the map. A burned-out cigarette hung from his mouth as he traced a route with his finger.

"Okay," he muttered. "We need to follow the road out of here, then turn down a side tunnel once we are out of town. We follow that tunnel for about three quarters of a mile, and we will hit the central tunnel."

"We'll get a move on in about three hours," Edwards said.

"Why then?" asked Stacey. "Why not right now? I'm ready to go!"

"If any part of the security detail is onto us, we'll find them before they find us, and besides, in a few hours, there will be people getting up and moving around town," Kennedy said. "The heat will lose us in the morning work rush."

"I anticipate more guards when we get to the central shaft, so the less conspicuously we can travel, the better," Edwards said. "And besides, we all need to get some rest."

Stacey walked over to where Kennedy was sitting and sat down beside him. She leaned against his shoulder and closed her eyes. He draped his arm around her, leaning his head against the wall. A smile crept onto both Kennedy and Stacey's face.

Edwards hung his head and sighed. He pulled his dog tags out of his shirt and raised the cross to his lips.

****

An hour and a half later, Edwards and Kennedy were sitting a few feet from the opening to the alley where they were hiding. Kennedy was smoking a cigarette, concealed in his fist, and Edwards was cleaning his fingernails with his Ka-Bar. A half-empty bottle of water sat near his leg.

"When I was just finishing basic," Edwards said, "the drill instructor told us to clean the barracks. Eddie Foster looked right at him and claimed he didn't know how. Damned kid asked the drill sergeant to show him how."

Kennedy chuckled. "Foster always was a smart-ass."

"It gets better," Edwards said. "He ran away. So there he goes, sprinting out of the barracks and went straight to PT yard. He did push-ups and burpees all day."

"Damn."

"That was before the drill sergeant got ahold of him. Guy made him scrub the entire barracks floor every day for a week with his toothbrush." Edwards stifled a laugh. He held a hand over his forehead and rubbed his eyes. "What the drill instructor didn't know was it was actually *his* toothbrush Foster was using!"

"Did that really happen?" asked Stacey, joining the men. She rubbed her eyes.

"Yeah," Edwards said. "Did Jason tell you about his time in Afghanistan?" He leaned over and punched Kennedy's shoulder.

She shook her head at him. Rubbing her eyes, she yawned and stretched.

"When I was overseas, I requested to work with Mike's unit," Kennedy said. "Served on quite a few patrols and even a couple of breaching operations. Luck was on my side, because on the day of Mike's last patrol, I had just been hurt. I got fourteen stitches and a groovy scar out of the deal. Anyway, I was getting my second round of dismissal papers from the US military that morning. Out of ten trucks to go out, three came back."

"I was in the last truck," Edwards said. "I did what I could for the men who survived that first round. After that it was just going from one dead man to the next. I can still see the men I lost that day yelling for the medic, screaming and crying. The ugliest face of war. That was honestly the single most horrible day of my life." He pulled the cross out of his shirt and held it to his lips for a moment. "I still can't sleep well at night. I'm lucky to get three hours at a time. It haunts me. Not in a PTSD kind of way, but more like a 'what could have happened' kind of way."

"I bet," Stacey said. "I'm sure both of you guys saw things over there that you wish you hadn't."

Edwards nodded. "Get some rest, guys. We still have quite a bit of ground to cover."

***

Edwards peered around the corner with Kennedy behind Stacey. They waited a full minute, then Edwards sprinted across the road. He waited a moment, and then let out a short whistle. Stacey followed him across and waited. She stopped next to Edwards and brushed a stray hair out of her face. Edwards repeated the whistle. Kennedy darted out into the street and heard the chirp of golf cart tires spinning on the road surface.

The golf cart whipped out into the road, straight ahead of Kennedy. Caught out in the open, he had nowhere to go. Kennedy looked around, finally settling a stare on the driver of the cart.

The passenger pulled a handgun out of the holster tucked under his left arm. He brought it up and held it in a single-handed ready position. The driver chuckled and floored the cart, steering it directly toward Kennedy.

"Come on, asshole!" Kennedy uttered through gritted teeth. He stood his ground, waiting for an indication of what the guard was going to do.

The golf cart barreled toward Kennedy, who appeared to be glacially calm. With less than twenty feet to go, a long whistle echoed off the buildings surrounding the street.

Kennedy ducked as a garbage can flew through the space he had occupied a moment before. He scrambled out of the way, just seconds before he would have been run down.

The can hit its mark, striking both men in the cart. Kennedy regained his feet and sprinted to where Edwards and Stacey were standing. A look of pain crossed his face for a moment as he caught his breath.

The guards had regained control of the golf cart and thrown the can and most of the garbage out of the front seat and begun to scan for Kennedy.

"Central, do you copy," the passenger said into a handset radio. "This is cart number seventeen. We have found the suspects, send backup."

"Copy that," the voice on the radio crackled.

"Time to go," Edwards said. He looked around. He spotted a nearby doorway and walked over to it. He tried the handle, only to find it locked. He kicked the door, splintering the wood. "Come on," he hissed and ducked inside. Stacey and Kennedy were close behind him.

***

Bethany was washing the morning dishes, her mind wandering. She thought about her husband, hoping to hear from him in the next couple of days. She knew the cellular reception would not be great where Edwards was, and she hadn't gotten a visit from anyone to tell her that Mike had been hurt, so she wasn't overly worried. The TV was on in the other room, a news program cut in and showed a photo of an older airplane sitting in front of a hanger.

"This just in," the anchor was saying seriously. "A local hotshot group, consisting of firefighters from Deer Ridge Fire Protection District and neighboring communities has been reported as missing. Preliminary reports show that it was last seen over the Erichson's Nature Preserve on-site to investigate a possible wildfire. There has been no contact with any on-site personnel, and the fire department has begun an investigation into the matter."

Bethany had shut off the sink, walked over to the half-wall that separated the kitchen from the living room, and watched the report, speechless. Tears began to well up in her eyes as she picked her cell phone up from the table and looked at it. The display showed no missed calls or messages, and she tried Edwards' number, her knuckles turning white from her grip on the device.

"Oh, please answer," she muttered. "Oh, please, oh, please answer!" The voice mail message kicked on just as soon as the call connected. She disconnected the call, sat down on the brown leather sofa in the living room, and flipped channels, trying to find another news broadcast with coverage of Edwards' plane.

She called the fire station and demanded to talk to Jefferson. He came on the line a moment later.

"Jefferson," he said into the phone.

"What the hell is going on? Where's Mike?"

Bethany said, her voice trembling as she spoke.

"Right now, I know as much as you do, Bethany." He sighed. "I got a call that their plane went down. As soon as I find out more, I'll call you."

"Thank you," she said and hung up. Her hands shook as she continued to flip through channels. Tears welled up in her eyes.

****

An overweight, middle-aged woman wearing a bathrobe sat watching the morning news on TV. Suddenly, the door splintered in on itself. She screamed as two men and a woman barged their way into her apartment, ran through it, and exited through the back door.

Edwards ran at the front, followed by Stacey and then Kennedy. They jogged down another large corridor. Edwards looked from one side to another, weighing options as he went. He noticed that the spacing of the doorways was widening, and the nameplates alongside them showed less offices and more storerooms. They had run for close to fifteen minutes when he started to slow.

"We need to stop!" Stacey called. "It's been a long time since I've jogged this much."

Edwards stopped and picked a door. He opened it and ducked inside, followed by Stacey and Kennedy.

"Now what?" asked Kennedy panting.

"Lock it," Edwards barked, swallowing hard.

"We're going to wait here for a while. Hopefully, we can lose some of this heat."

"Ugh," Stacey groaned. "More waiting around? I'm getting pretty sick of doing nothing."

"We can wait them out for a bit," Edwards said calmly. "There's a water cooler and a bunch of boxes. There's bound to be something useful in here."

Kennedy had already pulled a box down. He grinned as he pulled the top of the box off and pawed through it. Stacey walked over and peered into the box.

"This looks like promotional junk," she said. "Pens and key chains."

"Let's check a few more," Edwards said. He pulled a box down from a nearby shelf and opened it. He pulled out several boxes of stamped ink pens, then he sighed and shoved the box aside. "Nothing useful."

"Look at it this way, Mike," Kennedy said. "At least we have cold water available!"

"Yeah," Edwards said after a moment. "You got that map, Jason?"

"Yep," Kennedy said as he pulled the map out of his pocket. He opened it on the tabletop and smoothed the folds. He pulled out and lit a cigarette and exhaled a stream of blue smoke out of his nostrils.

"We're somewhere in here," he said, taking another drag and pointing. "The central shaft is here. We're getting fairly close now."

Edwards scrutinized the map for several minutes. He glanced up and looked Kennedy in the eyes. "I see a potential snag," he said at length. He pointed to a narrow spot in the tunnel.

"What is that?" asked Stacey.

"Security checkpoint," Kennedy said smirking. "I noticed that the first time we laid out this route."

"Oh, really?" Edwards asked snidely. "So what are we going to do about it?"

"I was going to do a thing," Kennedy said dismissively.

"A thing," Edwards repeated skeptically.

"Yeah, a thing. It was going to be a clever thing, but I suppose any old thing could work."

"What is so big a deal about a checkpoint?" Stacey asked. She had a look on her face that said she knew the answer but had to hear it spoken.

Edwards sighed heavily. He pulled the Ka-Bar out of its sheath and laid it on the table in front of him. He glanced from it to Stacey.

She glanced from the razor-sharp fighting knife to Edwards, then Kennedy, and back to the knife.

"Oh, I see. What are we going to do?"

"I don't know," Edwards admitted. He glanced at his bare wrist, then looked up, trying to find a clock. "We'll improvise. Sometimes an actual plan can be restricting."

Chapter Nineteen

Holly sighed heavily. The heavyset man was on the phone and glancing at a small notepad from time to time. He had already explained the situation to his superior twice and was then transferred. He had now been on the phone for nearly half an hour and was growing irritated.

"I told you, two men — smoke jumpers — are still inside," he said. "One was abducted, and the other one wandered into Wiln mine." A long pause, and then, "Yes, I understand that, sir. No sir, I don't think using civilians to do department dirty work is a wise career move. Agent Andrews told me who these men were and what they are capable of."

He fell silent, listening for a moment, then lowered the phone and grinned. "Damned reception, must've lost signal!" He sipped at the coffee in his hand and shook his head.

"Trust me, Johns," Holly said. "These guys are like a SWAT team, exfiltration specialists and demo team rolled into one. If anyone can do this without a full black ops team, it's those two."

"They understand the stakes?"

"These men will do the right thing," Holly said. "I know for a fact that between the two of them, those guys can talk, fight, run, and improvise their way out of any situation."

"Yeah, I still don't like it." He shook his head. "Do you have the documents?" He tucked the phone and notepad back into the pocket of his agency Windbreaker.

"Yeah, two problems," Holly said. "One: Mancirotti never once signed any memo nor any document that could possibly indict him in any kind of wrongdoing; Two: the documents that I do have that can prove wrongdoing are composite. There are so many different hands on it, it's like everyone in the office wrote one word and it was cut and pasted together, then photocopied. Even the ingrained identification of the printer has been removed. These guys are thorough."

"But there are documents, right?" Johns asked. "If we have nothing to go on, then we would have to arrest your smoke jumpers. If these guys are as good as you say, it'd be a shame to have to arrest them for trespassing."

"Don't worry, Johns," Holly said. "I trust those guys. I made sure they knew the score. Edwards and Kennedy both nearly fell over when I explained things. For God's sake, one is a combat veteran, and the other was a combat operator. I trust them. If anyone can pull this off, it's those guys."

A beep alerted Holly to a text message. She pulled her phone out and read the screen. A large smile crept across her face, and she responded to the message.

"I just got word from the men on the inside," Holly said. "They're getting close."

"Excellent," muttered Johns. "We'll arrange for an extraction team."

Holly unlocked the screen of her phone, keyed in a number, and waited while it connected.

"Hello," a singsong voice answered.

"Bethany Edwards? This is Holly Andrews with the FBI. I am going to send a car to pick you up."

"What's this about?" she asked. "Is Mike in trouble?"

"It is a long story, Mrs. Edwards," she said. "He is not in trouble. I'll have the agents fill you in on the way."

***

Bethany hung up and called Abbey over to her. "Sweetie, do you want to stay with Grandma?" Abbey's eyes widened, followed closely by her smile.

"Okay, go pack some toys, I'll call Grandma and have her come get you."

Abbey ran to her room, yelling excitedly the

whole way. Bethany had a concerned look on her face as she was calling her mother.

***

"Nice call on the cell, bro," Kennedy said. "Now what?"

"Here's what I'm thinking," Edwards said evenly. "You and Stacey are going to wait while I draw the guards away from the checkpoint. Once their attention is on me, you two run like hell, and we'll meet up here." He pointed to a spot on the map. It was an apartment building's lobby.

"Okay," Kennedy relented. "But, Mike, this is completely insane!"

"Noted," Edwards replied.

"I'm serious, dude," Kennedy said, not letting the conversation go. "You've got a family. It should be me. I'm willing to do this crazy-ass stunt of yours."

"With that ankle of yours?" Edwards asked. "There's no way. They'd catch you. I'm surprised you got into the firehouse with that."

"Think of Beth and Abbey!" he said. "Me, I'm a bachelor, I've got no attachments." He reached out and grabbed Edwards' shoulder. "I have nothing to lose. No kids that I know of. It should be me."

Stacey glanced at him, a concerned look on her face.

Edwards shook his head and stood. He walked across the room and doubled back on himself. He paced the room while speaking. "No, I'm going, that's it, case closed." He pulled the brass knuckles out of his pocket and flashed them at Kennedy. "I'll be alright."

"This is crazy, Mike," Stacey added. "You have a kid. You need to stay alive for her."

"I'm doing this for her," he said pointing. "So that way, my little girl will live in a world that is a little less corrupt. Besides, I was in Afghanistan when she was born. Bethany is more than capable, and there is a decent life insurance policy on me. They'll be fine."

Kennedy groaned and walked over to the water cooler. He took a cup from the tube on the side and filled it. He took a long sip and sighed. He leaned against the desk at the far end of the room. He rubbed a hand across his forehead and held his eyes shut for a moment.

He looked at the wall of boxes, each with its handwritten label. He was hoping something would jump out at him as being useful.

"Hey, Mike," Kennedy called. He walked to the shelf next to the door and reached up to the box on the top shelf. He brought it down and set it on the table. "Check out what I just found!"

He opened the clear plastic container and reached inside. He pulled out a flare gun with the H.C.Wiln Mining Company logo stamped on its side.

"What do you suppose this is dong in the middle of all this promo crap?" Kennedy asked.

"Maybe this will help you. *'Love C'*," Stacey read from the note taped to the side of the barrel. She dropped the note back into the box. "Sounds like a joke gift."

Edwards walked over and scooped up the flare gun. He looked it over and nodded. "What else do we have in these boxes?"

Chapter Twenty

"You sure about this?" asked Kennedy for the third time since they finalized the plan. The concern was etched on his face. "I told you, I'll go in your place. Hell, I'll go fight them off with my bare hands before I just let a man who is like a brother to me sacrifice himself.

"Yeah, Mike, we can figure out a better way," Stacey added. She put her hand on his shoulder.

"When you see the guards come after me, run like hell!" Edwards said. "Jason, if I—"

"Stop, you'll be fine," Kennedy interrupted. "Let's get this silly-ass plan of yours done. Stubborn bastard!"

Edwards sighed, slowly walking to the door. He opened it and trotted to the main hallway. He jogged toward the checkpoint.

The security checkpoint was situated in a natural bottleneck in the passageway. A small shack with a metal detector led to a gated crossing.

Three men worked at the checkpoint on alternating twelve-hour shifts.

Edwards, standing twenty feet from the guard shack, pulled a heavy brass paperweight out of his vest pocket. They found it in a box marked "Rewards for Outstanding Work". It had the words "Best Attendance" engraved on the plaque on the front. Edwards lobbed it at the checkpoint's door.

"Hell-ooo," he crowed. "I'm here to turn myself in!"

"What the hell?" the first guard out of the shack muttered. "Freeze!" he shouted as he drew his sidearm.

"I'm not running," Edwards said. His hands were clasped behind his back. The look of patient calm on his face belied how nervous he felt.

A second, then a third man exited the small shack. The largest of the three men took a step toward Edwards. "Put your hands over your head." the big man ordered.

Edwards stood and eyed all three guards. "You didn't say please," he quipped. He brought his hands around in front of himself, pointed the flare gun toward the guard shack, and squeezed the trigger.

The flare shot and shattered the window of the eight by fourteen foot room. A bright red glow erupted from the small building, and flames licked at the walls.

Edwards charged forward, the guards still

stunned from the suddenness of the attack. He shoulder checked the largest of the guards, knocking him off balance. The man fell, sprawling on the ground face first.

The second man, also distracted, was shoved to the tunnel floor. The final guard turned just as Edwards' brass-knuckle-wrapped fist swung hard toward his head. The man ducked just enough to avoid being knocked out. The guard countered with a hard rising knee to Edwards' midsection.

The hit drove the air out of Edwards' chest and caused him to stumble. He refused to go down and stumbled a step, sucking air in as fast as he could. Edwards was still struggling to take a full breath when he caught his balance. He forced himself into a sprint and shot past the guards. He bolted past the burning checkpoint building and ran down the corridor.

All three guards had regained their feet.

"You two, go find fire extinguishers!" the senior ranking guard ordered, pulling the radio handset off his belt. The other men scrambled, searching for fire extinguishers.

"Central command, this is checkpoint fourteen," he said into the radio. He brushed dust off the front of his uniform jacket and waited.

The radio crackled to life. "Go ahead, fourteen."

"This is John, at fourteen. One of the fugitives has eluded us."

"Copy that, fourteen," the dispatcher replied. "Word from Mr. Gonzales is to unleash the Sasquatch. Be advised. The handlers will be there in five."

"Roger, that, fourteen copies, wait for the Sasquatch and handlers." John shifted his weight uneasily. He watched as the checkpoint building burned.

****

Edwards ran until he couldn't breathe. He looked over his shoulder and saw no sign of being followed, then he looked around and found a door. As he threw the heavy steel door open, a long, unsettling creak sounding like a car sideswiping a bus. Edwards flinched and bound inside. He was greeted by a tangled mess of pipes and conduit running in all directions. Dim light from grimy fixtures cast deep shadows across the floor.

He shoved the door closed behind himself and felt the inside of the door for a lock. Not finding one, he crossed the room. Walking toward a dim light against the far wall, he found a workbench with a single lightbulb above it, and after scrounging around he found a length of pipe.

Edwards crossed back to the door and shoved the pipe under the door handle. It just happened to be the right length to block the door shut. He walked over and sat on a stool next to one of the boilers. Several paper coffee cups were strewn across the floor and nearby shelves, and an old stand-up ashtray was overflowing with burned-out cigarette butts. A pack sat on a nearby shelf and Edwards reached for it, finding a single cigarette inside. He lit it and waited.

***

"Uh, Jason," Stacey started, peering around the corner. "They're still there."

"Shit!" Kennedy said. "Really?"

"Yeah," she said sharply. "If you don't believe me, go take a look."

He glanced around the corner and saw all three men milling around the still-burning checkpoint. They were lamely trying to put the fire out.

"Okay," he murmured. He pulled the map out of his pocket, spreading it out as best he could. "Mike was going to wait for us here," he said, putting his fingertip on the red pen mark denoting their rendezvous point. "So if he had some issues, he would lay low somewhere."

"Are you sure he didn't just go straight to our meeting point?" asked Stacey.

"He wouldn't do that. He wanted to try to draw the heat away from us," Kennedy said. "He's hiding here," he said pointing.

"The boiler room?" Stacey asked. "Are you sure?"

"Of course. It's on a straight line from the checkpoint," Kennedy said. "At least we had better hope that is where he's hiding. You heard goon-squad radio."

She nodded and brushed a stray hair out of her face, her brown eyes wide. "We need to get past them."

Kennedy grinned a wild, toothy grin and spun on his heel. He backtracked two dozen feet and grabbed the fire extinguisher off the wall hook. He ran over to where the three guards were milling about.

"What's up, guys?" Kennedy said boisterously. "Need some help? I am a firefighter, you know!"

"No," John said. "Wait, who the hell—"

Kennedy squeezed the handle of the extinguisher, shooting a spray of dry chemicals into the guard's face. As he was starting to swing the nozzle, a shot rang out, and the man dropped to the ground clutching his knee. His head turned to the source of the shot, and he saw Stacey standing with the Colt still raised.

"Stacey! Move that ass!" Kennedy bellowed. He swung the empty extinguisher like a club and struck one of the guards in the temple. The man fell to the floor unconscious.

Stacey ran from their hiding spot and crossed the tunnel. As she was passing the checkpoint, Kennedy fell into step behind her.

"Freeze!" shouted the nearest guard, rubbing his eyes. He was just ahead of them.

Kennedy veered off and threw a devastating haymaker punch into the guard's face. He barely altered his stride as the punch landed. Kennedy's momentum combined with the force of the punch caused the guard to topple, falling hard to the tunnel floor. The man landed in a jumbled heap, not moving.

"So where did you learn to shoot like that?" Kennedy asked.

"My dad used to take me to the shooting range," she said blushing. "He would say, 'Stacey, a girl has to be able to take care of herself!' He taught me all kinds of things. I wish he were still around."

"I'm sorry to hear that," he muttered. "After we get out of here, I would like to take you to a nice little gourmet restaurant I know about—French cuisine, great ambiance, real nice place. They have a thousand-bottle wine cellar!"

"Thanks, but I'm more of a sports bar kind of girl. I'd rather go out for a pizza or hot wings and beer."

"I think I'm in love," he uttered.

***

Edwards studied the map, scrutinizing every available path. He scratched his chin and continued to stare. He had waited for close to ten minutes when a bang followed by the grind of steel stretched to its breaking point jarred Edwards back to reality.

An odor like wet fur and rotten meat filled the boiler room. A bellowing scream, high-pitched and long, echoed off the pipes and equipment.

Edwards searched frantically for a weapon. He found a length of rebar and picked it up. He knew the guards had found him with help from their nano-machine controlled Sasquatch.

As his right hand drifted to the ball chain around his neck, a light pull brought it out. He raised the steel cross to his lips and kissed it. Tears welled in his eyes. "I love you, Abby," he whispered. "Love you, Bethany. I am so sorry."

Heavy, thudding footsteps brought him back to the moment at hand and snapped him into reality as he prepared himself for anything. Shaking off the apprehension that was tightening his chest, he flexed his fingers and popped his neck while he waited.

***

Kennedy and Stacey were trailing fifty feet behind a group of guards. The men had heard the Sasquatch was out and hunting inside the facility, and they wanted to watch it kill a man. They chatted about it, as if it were no more than a baseball game.

"They got the Sasquatch tracking Mike," Kennedy whispered. "We need to get to him before they kill him." Pulling one of the larger wrenches from his pocket, he crept behind the closest man and hit him across the back of the head. The man fell to the floor silently. He dropped a second man with the same wrench and threw it to the floor, leaving it. Thirty feet ahead were three more guards, chatting obliviously.

***

The thudding footsteps drew closer, and Edwards stood his ground. The pipes he was hiding behind were suddenly wrenched free and thrown across the room. There standing in front of him, snarling and drooling, was the Sasquatch. It stood ten feet tall, and Edwards guessed it at well over five hundred pounds. It had large eyes and thick brow ridges and was covered head to toe with thick shaggy fur, and much of it was matted and mangy.

The stench wafting off the creature was enough to bring tears to Edwards' eyes. He started to breathe from his mouth. That didn't even help.

The large, hairy hands reached for him when a strong male voice yelled, *"Halt! Not for you!"*

The handler was a short, round man with thinning hair and a pasty complexion. The Sasquatch stopped, arms still raised. Two guards zipped past it, each one grabbing one of Edwards' arms. The man on his left side cuffed it to an overhead pipe-hanger. The man on the right wrapped Edwards' wrist tightly with a length of steel wire and twisted it around on itself.

"What the hell do you assholes want?" demanded Edwards. "This isn't in the brochure. I'd like to speak with the manager."

"We're paid to make sure this facility is secure," the man on the right said. "We get bonuses for enlisting volunteers."

"The nature preserve makes a great enlistment office," said the guard at Edwards' left side.

The handler cleared his throat. Both guards looked at him, then at each other.

"What do you think, Johnson, should he go vol-corp, or should we just kill him?" asked the guard at Edwards' left arm.

Oh, I don't know, Ryan," Johnson said. "I'm betting he'll escape. He is pretty quick."

Edwards blinked and steeled himself for whatever was coming. Ryan cleared his throat. "Throw him a beating," he ordered, glaring at the handler.

The handler smiled. "Beat him, keep him alive." The Sasquatch growled but followed orders. It drew a massive hand back, balled into a fist.

***

Kennedy and Stacey rounded the corner and saw the thick steel door crumpled and tossed aside.

"We're close," Kennedy said. Stacey was half a step behind him. He heard the quick hitch in her breathing.

"Come on," he said and crept closer. As he passed the destroyed door and looked around, he continued to walk past the door.

"Jason, over here," Stacey said, putting her hand on his shoulder. "I need you to calm down. You are no good to Mike or to me if you're in a panic or all emotional. I know he's your best friend, but come on, sweetie, pull it together."

He nodded and pulled the Colt .45 out of his waistband, and held it in a high ready position. As he walked slowly toward the open doorway, he closed his eyes and took a deep breath.

Standing in the doorway, he watched the activity inside. He crept up to the nearest guard, and using the butt of the handgrip struck the guard in the back of the head. As the guard stumbled forward and grabbed the door frame, Kennedy hooked his arm around the man's throat and pulled, but the guard held fast, refusing to let go.

Stacey walked over and kicked the guard hard in the groin. Kennedy shifted his grip a second before the kick landed, resulting in little more than a muffled groan.

Kennedy pulled the man over and kicked the guard hard in the head, knocking him out. As the guard fell in a crumpled heap on the floor between Kennedy and Stacey, he quickly pulled the cuffs off his belt and clicked them around the man's wrists.

"Think you could be just a little louder?" Stacey asked. Kennedy offered a half smile and raised his eyebrows.

"At least this one wasn't as loud as the guys who led us this far," Kennedy offered plainly. The only response he got out of Stacey was a head shake and eye roll.

He led the way into the next room and they made their way around it. The smell of rotting meat and damp fur assaulted them.

Kennedy yawned silently and raised his gun hand. Pressing the barrel of the handgun against the handler's head, he grabbed a handful of the man's shirt, spun him around, and then pressed the barrel into his forehead.

"Listen up, Chuckles," Kennedy growled. "Since you have the Sasquatch's ear, tell it to take out both guards holding my friend there."

The handler set his jaw and stared straight ahead. "If you kill me, the Sasquatch will kill your little friends, then turn on you."

Stacey leaned forward, pressing her lips against his ear. Kennedy watched as her jaw moved slowly, her eyes held closed. The handler swallowed hard. He uttered a few words in what Kennedy took as French. The Sasquatch snarled and lunged forward. A massive fist slammed into the first man's face, the sound of bone cracking resounding throughout the room. The second man tried to run. He screamed and tried to bolt past the Sasquatch. The Sasquatch caught the man as he was trying to run past and heaved him. The man slammed into the wall with a heavy thud, then landed in a crumpled heap and did not move.

Again, Stacey pressed her lips against the handler's ear and worked her jaw. He glared at her a moment, then swallowed and spouted an order in French.

The Sasquatch wheeled around on its heel and

punched the handler in the face, the man falling to the ground unconscious. The creature looked around and bolted out to the hallway, heavy feet slamming into the floor.

Stacey grinned wide and mischievously. "You are welcome. Someone has to take care of you boys. I swear sometimes you guys need a babysitter!"

"Thanks, hon," Kennedy said and crossed the room in three steps. He stopped in front Edwards and pressed his fingers to the side of his neck, looking for a pulse. "Oh, you wonderful bastard!" He placed a hand on his shoulder and gave him a light shake. "Mike, wake your lazy ass up, man."

Eyelids fluttered and opened slowly. "Kennedy, what are you doing?" Edwards spat and looked around. "You and Stacey get to the meeting point. I'll be there in a minute."

"You alright, Mike?" Stacey asked wide-eyed. She and Kennedy looked him over. "You're handcuffed to a pipe. You got beaten by the Sasquatch."

"Oh, right," he uttered. His right eye was swollen shut, and dark bruises were already starting to show across his face. His clothes were tattered in spots, and blood covered nearly every clean spot. Blood had dried on the sleeves of his shirt.

Stacey pulled the material away from his left wrist and saw that it had been bleeding. There was a thin trickle of blood running down his arm. She gently pulled the right side away and saw the wire and the ragged gash it had dug into his wrist. Peering at the left side, then the right, she decided the right side was by far the worst.

"Jason, one of these snoozing clowns should have a cuff key," Edwards said softly. "Find it, man, and let me down."

Kennedy snapped to attention and checked the nearest guard's belt. He searched in pockets and inside of pouches. "I don't think this one has a key."

"I'll check the other one," Stacey offered cheerily. She trotted over to the man and proceeded to check his pocket, belt pouches, and other hiding spots.

"Jason, main pocket of my IFAK, there is a tactical pen. Grab it."

"Mike, now isn't the time to make a grocery list," Kennedy said, but obliged.

As he pulled it out of the belt pouch, the pen rattled which caused Kennedy to shake it next to his ear.

"What have you got in here, Mikey?" Unscrewing the end, he upended the pen, and a cuff key fell out into his hand. He reached up, put the key into the hole, and turned it. As soon as Edwards' hand was free, it shot straight to his nose.

"That's better," Edwards said after scratching his nose for nearly a minute. "Damned nose started itching as soon as the goons put the lock on me. It was all I could think about for the last four days!"

"Mike, it's been about twenty minutes. At the most," Kennedy said. Stacey reached up, and using a pair of wire cutters she took from the tool bench near the other guard, she clipped the steel wire near the pipe. Kennedy caught his slumping friend and gently lowered him to the floor.

He looked at his wrists and reached for the IFAK on his belt, wincing as he did so. The deep gash bled freely as he tried to regain the strength to stand up.

"Don't you dare try to stand up," Stacey said and opened the first aid kit. "What do you need? How do we help you?"

"Need a roll of thick gauze, tape, and a couple of aspirin," he ordered, and Stacey complied. She removed a pair of aspirin from a bottle and dropped them in Edwards' left hand. He dry-swallowed the medicine and coughed. "Okay, my head feels a bit fuzzy, but that should be expected. I'm not nauseous, and I don't think I have a concussion. That's good. How deep is that cut on my wrist?"

"It's pretty bad," Stacey offered. "I'd think you needed stitches, but I don't know anything about this stuff." She had a look of concern etched on her face.

"If I need stitches then we're pretty well in trouble," Edwards snapped. "I can't suture worth a shit left-handed. If it's life or death, I'd give it a shot, but I don't think it'll be my best work."

"Mike, take a deep breath, man, you're shaking," Kennedy said. "We need you to calm down. Neither of us has any clue what to do."

"It's shock from blood loss and getting my ass kicked by a Sasquatch. Take the gauze and wrap my wrist. Put three or four layers on it, and tape it in place."

"The wire cutting into your wrist," Stacey asked, "what do we do about it?"

"Leave it. It's stopping the bleeding a little bit," Edwards said. "I can't tell how deep it actually is. It probably won't be enough for me to bleed out, but it will be enough to screw with me."

"How so?" she asked.

"Nausea, light-headedness, and if I lose enough blood, possibly coma," he rattled off. "Not in a spot to push my luck."

Stacey started to wrap the gauze around Edwards' wrist, but it kept slipping. Her hands were shaking nearly as much as Edwards'. Kennedy walked over and held the end in place. Stacey ran the gauze roll around his wrist a second then a third time, and Kennedy taped it, wrapping it three times.

"How's that, Mike?" Kennedy asked. He looked over and saw that Edwards' head was down, chin resting against his chest. Panic rose in Kennedy's chest until he heard his friend snoring.

"Stace, when he wakes up, he needs to know

we have to scrap this vigilante crap," Kennedy said and sighed. "He needs to go to a hospital. I know for a fact he won't go for it, but it's worth trying. He wants to nail the son of a bitch in charge to the wall. At this point, he'll be getting off lucky at that."

"I know he will," Stacey said. "You guys would move the world to do the right thing."

"All I can say is if Mike dies here, I'll beat the son of a bitch in charge to death!" Kennedy said, eyes blazing.

"I know," Stacey said. "I'd let you."

"Where the hell did the Sasquatch go?" asked Kennedy. "And what the hell did you tell the handler?"

"I told him the truth. If you got ahold of him, you'd not only kill him but also the Sasquatch. Told him you were absolutely insane. I sent him into the woods. He's searching for a yeti to play tag with." Stacey laughed.

CHAPTER TWENTY-ONE

The phone trilled, and a groan was audible over the sound. A meaty hand reached out and tapped the button for the speakerphone. "Gonzales."

"Sir, this is checkpoint fourteen, calling from checkpoint twelve. The fire is out, but we haven't been able to find the firefighter."

"Of course not," scoffed Gonzales. He lifted and dropped the receiver back onto the cradle, severing the connection. He propped his elbows onto the desk, rubbed his temple, and finally sat pinching the bridge of his nose for several minutes. Finally opening his eyes, he sat upright and stretched his thick neck as far back as it would go. He stared at the ceiling, then snapped back into reality. He pulled out a facility map and plotted a course based on sightings, then discarded any sighting that did not involve one of his men being assaulted.

"All free and off-shift security personnel, meet at briefing room six," he said into his radio. "One hour!" He tossed the radio onto the desk with a bang and smiled to himself, chuckling. "I'm on to you, firemen!"

***

Edwards bolted upright. He had slept for over three hours and was a little groggy. The swelling that blocked out the vision in his right eye had gone down by about half, and he was able to see in a squint. He looked at both wrists and saw a square of gauze taped in place on his left wrist and the bandage job on his right arm, and he smiled. The bandage was still white, but he knew it wouldn't stay that way for long.

"You guys did a fantastic job of bandaging me up," Edwards said. Kennedy nodded. He was sitting by the door, Colt sitting out and on the floor next to him. Stacey dozed on the other side of him, her head on his leg. "How long have I been out?"

"About three hours," Kennedy said. He pulled a cigarette out of the pack and offered one to Edwards. Edwards nodded and tried feebly to catch the pack as it was tossed in his direction. "Lighter's in the pack."

"Thanks," he said as he picked up the pack and lit a cigarette. He exhaled the smoke. "If I hadn't shifted my arm when I did, I'd have to learn how to write all over again. It'll be sore in the morning, that's for sure."

Kennedy nodded. Edwards stood slowly. He was stiff but still able to move. He swung his upper body first one direction then the other, eliciting a series of pops all along his back and a couple from his sternum. "Let's go!" Edwards said. "If we wait any longer, I'm going to stiffen up, and it'll take a truck to move me."

Kennedy nudged Stacey, who woke slowly. "Wake up, Stace, we need to get moving."

"Okay," she murmured.

Fifteen minutes later, all three were gathered at the door. Kennedy turned the handle and led the way down the hallway. Edwards was at the end and was walking with a slight limp.

"You good, Mike?"

"I'm fine, Jason," he answered, gritting his teeth. "Just enjoying a leisurely stroll. I may have a couple of broken ribs from our big hairy buddy."

They continued to move through the hallways toward the offices of the central shaft. Making good time, they arrived at a junction. A sign on the wall pointed an arrow at the hallway on the right, toward maintenance. The left side was labeled "Central Elevators."

"Looks like we're going this way," Stacey said pointing.

"Nope, we're going this way," Edwards said and pointed. A wild grin plastered across his face.

"Are you sure?" asked Kennedy.

Edwards shrugged. "The shortest distance

between two points is a straight line. Plus, while I was waiting for the Sasquatch, I found a maintenance diagram. Trust me."

"You crazy son of a bitch!" Kennedy said smiling. Edwards grinned in response and reached up to the dropped ceiling. He pushed and slid a tile up and out of the way.

"Okay, Stacey," Edwards said. "Up you go."

She placed a foot into Edwards' hands and was easily lifted up into the ceiling. He repeated the process with Kennedy who reached down and pulled Edwards up with one hand.

The ceiling tile had just dropped back into the overhead track when two guards on patrol rounded the corner. They walked through the corridor that Stacey and the firefighters had just occupied.

The firefighters clambered up onto a rock wall. The wall was utilized as the back wall of the offices and storerooms on this particular floor. Three feet wide and chiseled flat on top, it acted as a natural maintenance walkway. They used the walkway to cross the hallway completely unobserved.

A steel wall ran across the opening, providing support for the floor above. A four-foot square steel panel in the center was the only access point to the elevators. Edwards pulled a wrench from his back pocket and handed it to Kennedy.

"Take that panel off, and we can get to the elevator," he ordered.

Kennedy adjusted the wrench to fit the bolts, and after a few minutes had the panel off and sitting on the stone walkway. As they ducked through the opening, Edwards clicked on a flashlight, shining it ahead.

Edwards turned and held a hand up. He listened and faintly caught the sound of feet in the hall, less than six feet away from where he stood. The conversation was muted, just to the point of being indiscernible.

"Security is in the hall for central shaft elevators," Edwards whispered. He started forward again but stopped when Kennedy grabbed his arm.

"What is the plan?"

"We are going to have a word with the boss," Edwards whispered. "Pay attention. We're going to see what we can wrangle up."

"It plays to our skill of getting into trouble," Kennedy admitted. "How?"

"We'll just take the elevator," he said evenly. A bemused smile crossed his beaten face, and he winked. "Unless you want to take the stairs."

Edwards turned and continued forward. Moving slow and cautiously, he crept along the rock walkway. He shot glances to both sides, and from behind it looked as if his head were mounted on a swivel. He came to a stop and turned around, grinning like a Cheshire cat. He held his arms straight out at his shoulders.

"Here we are, the elevator," he said. "We got

lucky, it's right where we need it!"

Without saying another word, Edwards leaped across the gap and landed on the cab of the elevator. Stacey stepped over to the edge, saw the nearly six-foot gap, and swallowed.

"I'll never make it across," she said. "It's too far."

Kennedy stepped over to her and placed his big hands on her waist. He lifted her with ease. "Sorry, hon, this won't be real nice," he uttered as he tossed her over the gap and onto the elevator cab. Edwards caught her as she landed.

She had just opened her eyes when a muffled ding sounded from inside the cab, and the elevator lurched upward.

"Jason!" Stacey called as the cab rose above the tunnel roof.

"Shit," muttered Kennedy. As he sat down with his legs crossed, he placed his elbows on his knees and rested his chin in his hands, watching as the thick steel cables running on either side of the elevator shaft first stopped then reversed. He calmly watched as the elevator came back into view. A knot of apprehension formed in his stomach as the elevator settled back in position without Edwards or Stacey on top of the cab.

He stood, taking a step back. As he jumped, barely clearing the gap, he caught himself on the edge of the car and lifted himself the rest of the way up. Searching the top of the car, he looked for an emergency hatch but couldn't find a handle of any kind. There was limited lighting in the elevator shaft, and his lighter was inside the cigarette pack in a buttoned shirt pocket.

The door banged open behind him, causing Kennedy to start. He quickly looked for an out, when he saw a head poke out of the car.

"Jason, get your ass in here," Edwards said laughing. "All the bought air is gettin' out!"

Kennedy dropped into the car. "What kept you, Mike?"

"Oh, you know women," Edwards said. "Stacey wanted to do a little shopping." He slipped the brass knuckles back into the cargo pocket of the guard's pants he had stolen. He was wearing a crisp white shirt as well. "I had a little trash to take out, and I needed to get a new shirt."

"Wow," Kennedy muttered. "We're in the middle of an escape and you stop to change your shirt. Your other one was barely even dirty!"

"It wasn't me this time," Stacey said. "It was all him. We didn't even go to any of the stores I wanted to shop at."

"Vanity issues," Edwards said and smirked. "Besides, this little number brings out my eyes." He reached out and tapped a button on the control panel, and the elevator began to rise.

Chapter Twenty-Two

Gonzales shook his head and watched the feed a third time. It showed the three people he was looking for in the central shaft elevator. The clip ran for over a minute until the larger of the men stepped over to the camera and slammed the butt of his handgun into it, causing the feed to stop. He slid the bottom left drawer open and pulled out a steel lockbox. He entered the combination and opened the top.

Hefting the large frame weapon, he sighed. "You three have forced my hand." Gonzales set the handgun, a .50 Desert Eagle, onto the top of his desk. Walking across the office, he plucked the shoulder holster off a coat stand in the corner. He pulled the holster on as he crossed back to the desk and slid the weapon into the holster.

Just shy of fifty, Gonzales spent as much time in the gym as his work schedule allowed and had the body of a man twenty years his junior. When he was not coordinating the security efforts around the mine, he was working out in the gym.

"How the hell a couple of firemen can evade my elite security men is beyond me," he said aloud. "Pure, dumb luck." The tone of his voice did nothing to convince him, and he had an uneasy feeling in the pit of his stomach.

He walked briskly from his office to a set of stairs winding up a level. At the top of the stairway was a steel door with a card reader. He swiped his card and entered. The entire floor was dedicated to posh executive offices and conference rooms. Here there was no indication of the structure being entirely underground. He approached Mancirotti's office and knocked at the door.

"Come," came a shout. Gonzales opened one side of the double doors and entered sheepishly.

The office was huge, at least thirty feet long and nearly twenty feet wide. A massive oak desk stood in the center near the back wall. An extensive bookcase sat against one wall. On the opposite side sat an old, worn-out minivan seat.

"Yes, Mister Gonzales?" asked Mancirotti. "Something I can help you with?"

"Mister Mancirotti, sir, I think the firefighters are coming here," Gonzales said meekly.

"Gather what men you can, and see if you can work out the situation," Mancirotti said. "I can't imagine this is out of your area of expertise, is it?"

"Yes, sir," Gonzales said and turned on his heel.

He walked out of the office as briskly as he could. "I'll handle it, sir."

"Do what it takes," Mancirotti said. "Just make sure it's handled."

***

"Did you find anything useful on the way, Jason?" asked Edwards. "I still have the flare gun, a couple of flares, and a wrench."

"I've got this," Kennedy said and pulled the Colt .45 out of his waistband and held it up.

"We can work with that," Edwards said thoughtfully. "It'd be nice to have a few flash-bangs or something."

"A couple more bodies, each with a gun would be nice," Kennedy offered. "Or maybe a tank. You know every security guard in this place will be in the boss's office."

"I'd be happy with a clown holding a baseball bat," Edwards said. "But since that neither makes sense nor is remotely possible given the circumstances, we may have to improvise."

Edwards pulled the map out of his pocket and studied it. He tapped the stop button and waited a moment, then returned his attention to the map.

"Here is the security storeroom, armory, and training area," Edwards said pointing. "Let's see if we can cause some trouble there. Maybe even do a little shopping and rearranging. I think if we put our minds to it, we could really feng shui things!"

"You, know, Mike, I really think we can find us

some trouble," Kennedy said.

"It is what you guys do best," Stacey said. "That's why I'm here, to keep you guys from getting into too much trouble."

"Good luck with that," snorted Kennedy. "That really is a full-time job, you know, and we still manage to find trouble."

Reaching out, Edwards keyed the button, causing the car to lurch and climb. Stacey looked from one man to the other and saw a grim determination on both their faces.

"So what is the plan on this one?" she asked.

"Honestly, I haven't got a clue," Kennedy said smiling.

"That makes two of us," Edwards added. "But I know there'll be trouble!"

The display on the elevator panel indicated the car had reached the twenty-third floor. Two floors above them was Mancirotti's office. A resounding ding notified them they had reached their destination.

"Here we are," Edwards said. "Time for another little shopping trip!"

As they exited the elevator and stepped into a locker room, they walked cautiously through to the other side and entered a short hallway. A bunk room stood on one side of the hall and a locked door on the other. A small gray box next to the handle told Edwards they needed a card key.

"Shit, Jason, did you happen to lift an ID badge

from one of the guards?"

"No, Mike, how about you?"

The men heard a shuffle behind them and looked back. Stacey stood with her hand out, an ID badge sitting on her palm.

"Here you go, geniuses," she said. She stepped forward and tapped the card against the reader. The red light on the top of the reader did not change color. A second tap only illuminated a second red light.

"I don't know what the deal is," Stacey said. "I found this card over there sitting on the first bunk."

"What's it say on it?" asked Kennedy.

"It has a name on it—Derek Williams—and under that it says 'In Training'."

"You don't suppose this is for specific guards, do you?"

As Stacey was reaching down to tap the card for the third time, Kennedy grabbed the Ka-Bar off his hip in an underhand grip. He swung his fist at the card reader, burying the seven inch blade to the hilt through both the card and card reader. A beep sounded and faded. They waited, expecting an alarm, but none sounded. Kennedy tried the door handle, only to find it still locked.

A sharp kick right next to the door handle caused the wood door to flex but not give. Kennedy swore under his breath and kicked a second, then a third time. Three kicks were enough to cause the door to give up and splinter in on itself.

"Okay, Jason, if you would like to go and grab the stuff on the list, Stacey and I will wait in the car."

"No impulse buys!" Stacey called after him smiling. "Check prices before you just grab things."

Kennedy walked into the armory and felt like a kid in a candy store. He grabbed an armful of flash grenades, then looked around. He saw a bin marked *.45 ACP* and grabbed a pair of preloaded clips for his Colt and slid them into a pocket. He picked up some duct tape and a length of para-cord. He filled a backpack, and slung it onto his back. Taking a pair of flash grenades, he duct taped them to the wall on either side of the door. Pulling the inner strands out of the para-cord, he tied both end to the pins, making sure it was tight. Smiling to himself, he left the armory, being careful to step over his trap. He clicked the light off and walked over to the elevator.

***

Gonzales stood at the back of the group. Close to twenty-five guards milled about in the hallway outside of Mancirotti's office. Idle chatter was beginning to start, and many of the men had sat down, either in the waiting room style chairs off to one side or on the floor. One man was chatting up the receptionist whose desk was halfway between the elevator and the back room. Gonzales was shaking his head. He made a mental note to hold a training meeting on protocol while on the clock.

The elevator dinged, indicating that the car had arrived. The doors sat not moving for several minutes. A chill ran up Gonzales's back.

"Look alive!" barked Gonzales. "Be ready!" The doors still hadn't opened, nor did the car move. The group of security guards waited for close to three minutes.

"Open it," Gonzales snarled. Three big men trotted forward. The men stacked up, one on either side and one at the control panel. The men stood there watching as the man at the controls tried tapping the button, then looked at it for a moment.

"Use the bypass!" shouted Gonzales frustrated. The guard, a man named Quinn, dug in his pocket until he found his bypass key. He put it into the port on the control panel and turned it. A red light clicked on, indicating they had control at that panel. He keyed the button for the doors and waited a heartbeat. Slowly, the doors slid open.

A mass of confusion, followed by several concussive thumps and bright flashes of light issued from the elevator car, was causing disorientation among the guards.

"Find those assholes!" bellowed Gonzales rubbing his eyes. "Kill them."

***

Willem Mancirotti sat at his desk, browsing through a stack of R and D reports. He had a steaming mug of coffee sitting next to his left side from which he took the occasional sip, and a large cigar sat perched in a heavy antique brass ashtray on the right side of the desk. A handful of photographs in frames sat on the perimeter of the desk showing his two children—now grown—as kids, one playing soccer, the other at a ballet recital. Soft classical music played from hidden speakers all around the room. A large fish tank housing several exotic species was set into the wall to the left of Mancirotti's desk.

Mancirotti lifted the cigar, a Havana, and puffed on it. He blew the strong-smelling smoke toward the ceiling and watched as it swirled against the ceiling tiles. He smiled and returned his attention to the reports on his desk. As he took a long sip of coffee and was looking over the latest information, a smile crossed his face.

Suddenly a load bang followed by the sound of men's voices came from the outer office. A monitor showing the feed from a hastily installed camera sat on his desk, and glancing at it, he saw the guards milling about, many holding their eyes and the rest pressing into the men in front of them to get a look into the elevator. Mancirotti shook his head and tapped a button inset into the top of his desk, powering the electromagnetic door lock.

The office was constructed like a bank vault with three-inch-thick steel walls on two sides, and the other sides bedrock. The steel door was locked via standard key and electromagnets from the inside. In events like this, there was no way to force entry into the office.

Mancirotti leaned back, puffing on his cigar and watching events unfold in his outer office. Suddenly a ceiling tile exploded out of the suspended track between the desk and the door. A man dropped to the floor, followed by a woman, and then a second, larger man.

"Willem Mancirotti," boomed the first man. "You are under citizen's arrest."

"Who the hell are you?" asked Mancirotti, calmly puffing on the cigar. "And why am I under arrest? What are the charges?"

"My name is Mike Edwards," answered the first man, "and these are my associates, Stacey Cartwright and Jason Kennedy. You are under arrest for conspiracy, kidnapping, manslaughter, extortion, and a few other things I'm sure my federal agent friends can come up with."

"So what, you three are federal agents?"

"No, if we were, we'd arrest you like federal agents would, with a lot of men in black gear and rifles," Kennedy said grinning. "And there'll be Miranda rights and me not beating the shit out of you. We ain't feds."

Stacey walked over and snapped the physical door lock shut while Kennedy pulled the Colt 1911 out of his waistband. He made a show of dropping the clip out of the handgrip, checking it, and sliding it back in. He pulled the slide back and lowered it to his side, pointing at the ground.

"Tell me why I shouldn't have my security men come in here and kill you," said Mancirotti calmly.

"Easy, boss-man," Edwards said holding up his hands. "Just gotta tell you, I cut the line for your intercom. And the phone. Yeah, I am such a klutz, it just sort of slipped. My bad!"

"What do you want? Money?" demanded Mancirotti. "I will not pay for silence, there will be no blackmail money for you idiots. My security detail will be sure you will not speak of my business."

"You have one hell of an office security system. Solid steel, electromagnetic locks," Edwards said. "Damned near impregnable. Except from the access point in the maintenance tunnels. Pretty big oversight."

"I'll let my people know," Mancirotti muttered. "You three will never know about it though."

"You seem to misunderstand," Stacey said. "My boys here just want to do the right thing. They want this place shut down. Now there is a big difference between them. Mike wants you to stand trial and pay for what you've done. Jason, well, he's a little more eye for an eye." She laid a hand along the side of her mouth, and in an exaggerated stage whisper said, "Jason is a little...unhinged."

"I think you should catch a beating from your Sasquatch first," Kennedy growled. "Then who knows, see where it takes us from there. If I get my way, you'll never see the light of day again."

"Jason used to be a combat operator," Edwards said. "Sometimes he reverts back to that violent mindset. Of course, he always has been a hothead, and has never been afraid of a fight, regardless of numbers." He clamped his hand on Kennedy's shoulder and looked seriously at Mancirotti. "He's a little crazy!"

"Of course," Mancirotti dismissed. "There is one in every group, however, I fail to see the part where I should care."

"Anyway, getting back on track, I want to see you defamed, and all the money you have made doing this will go into a fund to begin reparations to the families you destroyed."

"How noble," Mancirotti said. "But unfortunately, I have the means to make you simply disappear."

"Yeah, I know," Stacey said slowly. "I was a part of your volunteer corps for four days. I'm sure not going back there. If I have to drag you out of here myself, this operation is going to be shut down."

Mancirotti looked Stacey over and smirked. "You are feisty, I'll give you that. Hell, I like that in a woman. It will take far more than you and your hulking, monosyllabic friends here. I have a security force comprised of highly trained professionals. Most of those men are former Special Forces. Try it."

Smirking, Kennedy strode over to the desk and

opened the desktop humidor, pulling out a couple of fine cigars and holding them up so Edwards could see. He slid two into the pocket on his shirt. A third one stayed clutched in his hand.

Standing resolutely, Edwards tossed a pair of handcuffs on the floor ten feet from the desk. "Put these on, Willem."

"Now why in hell would I do that?" asked Mancirotti. "Is this guy serious? Those are actual Cubans, and they are very expensive. Do you mind?"

Kennedy bit the end off the cigar and spat it at Mancirotti. "Not at all, love a cigar. Smoke 'em if you got 'em!" He pulled his blue plastic lighter out of his pocket, eliciting a scowl from Mancirotti, who shoved a box of stick matches toward him.

"Security!" shouted Mancirotti.

"Not going to work, Willem," Stacey said sweetly. "You see, most of your security force has been called away. A friend called in that we were robbing her. A corporate lawyer. Very nice woman. Apparently it was an armed robbery, and we refused to leave. There should be a pretty heated standoff right about now."

"Just to clue you in, she was also doing a bit of moonlighting," Edwards said. "She's a federal agent. She has enough dirt on you to put you away for the rest of your life."

Mancirotti's eyes gave away nothing, as if he had already known. He glowered at the man smoking one of his cigars.

"Willie," Kennedy said. "Can I call you Willie? Anyway, how about you go ahead and put those handcuffs on before I beat the living piss out of you and cuff your left hand somewhere you won't find overly dignifying. Sound like a plan, Willie?"

"I don't think so," Mancirotti said haughtily. "And if you must, it's Willem."

Edwards walked over and grabbed a cigar out of the desktop humidor. Sitting on the edge of the desk, he used the shiny cigar cutter and lit the Cuban.

After a couple of drags, he dropped the cigar on the floor. "Ugh, Jason, this thing tastes terrible! How the hell are you still smoking yours?" He brought his booted foot onto the still-burning cigar, crushing it into the carpet. A flash of anger crossed Mancirotti's face.

"There are feds waiting for you," Edwards said. "You are going to prison for a very long time, Willem. Now, if I were you, I'd come with us before those guys decide to go spec ops and blast their way inside. I have no idea what is going on topside. For all I know, they have a team of men ready to rout your security team and arrest your miserable ass. Hell, you may go down in a hail of bullets. Given what I've seen, that may just be a fitting end for you."

Kennedy wandered around the office, randomly picking things up and purposely fumbling the breakables. He stopped at the fish tank, pressed his nose against the glass, and tapped at it a couple of times. Mancirotti scowled the whole time. He ashed on the carpeting and did all he could to irritate Mancirotti.

Stacey, who had been hanging back, walked to the middle of the office, picked up the handcuffs, and snapped them onto Mancirotti's wrists.

"This'll never stand up in court!" Mancirotti spat. "I have so many lawyers, I'll sue you until your grandkids pay out their noses! You'll never hold down a job again."

While Mancirotti was yelling and threatening legal action, Edwards crossed back to the hole in the ceiling. He reached up and pulled a hanging strap. A backpack dropped out. He retrieved a roll of duct tape and pulled a strip off, then he pressed it over Mancirotti's mouth.

"Alright, Willem, time to go," Stacey said as sweetly as she could.

"Is there a way out?" Edwards asked. "I know a bigwig like you would probably have a secret entrance."

Mancirotti refused to make eye contact until Stacey leaned in close and pressed her lips against his ear. The firefighters watched her jaw working and a look of panic crossing her face. Kennedy ripped the tape off, eliciting a groan from Mancirotti.

"Behind my desk, it's a false wall," he blurted.

"Leads out into a cinder block shed in the middle of the woods."

"Jason, if you would be so kind as to lead the way," Edwards said.

"It'd be my privilege," Kennedy said. "And, might I add, you have been a dream to work with on this lovely little project."

"Boys," Stacey interrupted, "let's just get the hell out of here!"

CHAPTER TWENTY-THREE

"Where the hell are your guys at?" demanded Johns as he was pacing impatiently. He looked from the watch on his wrist to the display on his phone, clenching in his right hand.

"They'll be here," Holly answered. The agents stood at the front of a group of black SUV's parked in a semicircle around the cinder block building used for supply drops. "I just received word they were on their way out with Mancirotti."

"As far as I know, this is the only way in or out of Wiln Mine," she said. "It has to be here."

"No, it doesn't, Holly!" a voice called from behind the SUV's.

"How the hell?"

"Willem, here, has his own private entrance," Edwards said as he shoved Mancirotti forward. The handcuffs were tight on his wrists, and it looked as if he had fallen a few times. His clothes were filthy and disheveled. "He had a rough time, hiking the three and a half miles here. You fell what, like ten times?"

"I think it was closer to twenty," Kennedy said smirking, "Those fancy-assed shoes are no good out here in the woods. Good thing we were with him."

"My lawyers will have a field day with this," Mancirotti said as he was led away by a federal agent. "You idiots are going to be in deep trouble."

"So how about some medical attention for Mike and a ride home?" asked Kennedy.

"First, you need to answer a few questions," Johns said puffing his chest up.

"Can I at least call my wife?" Edwards asked, exhaustion creeping into his voice.

"Not until we debrief you," Johns said. "Some of this may be sensitive information."

"Okay, two things, asshole," Edwards growled. "One: I know for a fact there was media coverage of at least some of this. Mainly because I helped arrange it; two: I'm sure my wife has been going bat-shit crazy with worry. So if you would be so kind as to allow me a few minutes to let my wife know I'm still alive, I'd greatly appreciate it. Relatively minor ask, considering we did your damned job for you on this one!"

Johns stared at him for a minute, then shook his head. "Can't allow it, tough guy." He hitched up his pants and stood resolutely.

"Me and Jason accomplished in a few days

what you and your people couldn't in months," Edwards said. "We even brought out an eyewitness."

Kennedy, standing within earshot of the whole exchange, walked over and stepped up to Johns. He bumped into Edwards and placed a hand on his shoulder. Turning to the agent, they stared eye to eye until Johns blinked.

"Mike is going to call his wife, amigo," Kennedy said tersely.

"Absolutely not!" said Johns firmly. "The EMTs need to check him out, and he needs to be debriefed."

Kennedy swung a hard punch into John's forehead, the brass knuckles adding to the power behind the punch. Johns fell to the ground, dazed.

Holly put her hands up and signaled all the agents that everything was fine. She put her hand on Edwards' shoulder. "There is no need, she's here." She spoke softly into a radio and smiled. "She's on her way."

Bethany was sitting in one of the black SUVs when the agent behind the wheel turned to her. "Your husband is here," he said, deadpan. He pointed out the windshield, toward a group of people standing near an ambulance.

She threw the door open and ran, shoving past an agent and ignoring everything around her.

She leaped into Edwards's arms, tears streaming down her face. "Mike! I thought you were dead!" she sobbed. "Oh my God! I am so happy to see you!"

"Hey, hon," he said, "we need to go to the hospital."

"Why?" she asked wiping her eyes. "Oh my God, are you alright, what happened?"

"It's a long story," he said with a smile on his face, "I'll tell you on the way."

Kennedy and Stacey stood together while Edwards was reunited with Bethany. He slid the brass knuckles into his pocket.

"So, what did you tell Mancirotti to change his mind?" Kennedy asked.

"I told him that you were as crazy as an outhouse rat," she said, "and that you were already on the verge of snapping. One of your triggers was obstinate CEOs."

He laughed and pulled her close, kissing her passionately.

***

As Edwards sat on the hospital bed waiting for the ER doctor to suture his wrist, Kennedy and Stacey sat in the waiting room. They chatted back and forth for several long minutes, when Bethany walked over to them. She handed each of them a cup of coffee.

"Jason, how's Mike?" she asked. "They finished with him yet?"

"He's in bay three," Jason answered.

"He's been arguing with the ER staff since you

left," Stacey added. "They'll be glad when he leaves!"

"That figures," Bethany laughed. "That man knows his stuff. He'd be a doctor except for the schooling."

"Yeah," she said. "Mike and Jason saved my life. I owe both of them my life!"

"Bay three?" Bethany asked. Stacey nodded and watched as she walked through the doors. She rounded the corner and stepped over to Edwards' side.

"Mike," she said seeing his wrist, "how are you doing?"

"Peachy," he muttered. "Did you bring me a coffee?"

"Sure did!" She leaned over and kissed him. The ER doctor cleared his throat. Bethany looked over. "Sorry."

She sat in the chair near the foot of the bed and watched as the doctor stitched Edwards' wrist and applied a clean dressing. Edwards watched the doctor.

After receiving discharge instructions, Bethany walked out to the waiting room with Edwards a step behind her. She stopped next to Kennedy and Stacey. "Do you have a ride?" she asked.

"No, would you be willing?" Kennedy asked.

"Absolutely. Come on," she said. "You too, Stacey."

Epilogue

Mike and Bethany Edwards sat on the beach, Mike sipping a cold beer while they watched Abbey playing in the gentle waves. She darted in and out of the water, giggling as she did.

Edwards sighed. "This is great, isn't it?" He glanced at the jagged scar on his right wrist. "I don't think today could get any better."

"Definitely," Bethany said, snapping photos of their daughter playing. The DSLR camera clicked nearly constantly. Edwards looked over to his right and saw Jason and Stacey sitting together, each with a drink. Stacey wore a tasteful two-piece bathing suit with a floral print cover, and large framed sunglasses sat on the nearby table.

"Mike, this is great!" Jason crowed. "I'm glad we started our business."

Stacey yawned and stood up. "Anyone need another drink?"

Both men held their empty beers out as she walked over to the bar. Kennedy looked over at

Edwards and winked. A few moments later, Stacey returned, dropped Mike's beer off, and returned to her chair.

"Get up, Stace," Kennedy said. She obliged and he took her hand in his, a wild smile on his face. He reached into the pocket of his board shorts.

"What are you doing?" Stacey asked. Kennedy suddenly dropped to one knee, her hand in his.

"Stacey Cartwright, will you marry me?" he asked.

She was speechless for a full minute. "I, uh, yes! Oh my God, yes!" He slid a diamond engagement ring onto her finger. She stared for a minute, then walked over to where Mike and Bethany sat.

"Bethany," she squealed and held her hand out for her to see." Jason just proposed to me!"

"Congratulations, guys!" Edwards said. "About time you settled down, Jason. Congratulations, Stacey!"

Abbey ran over and jumped into Edwards' lap.

"Guess what, kiddo?" he said. "Uncle Jason is going to get married to Stacey!"

"Yay!" Abbey laughed. "Aunt Stacey, Uncle Jason!" She clapped and hopped back down, running away.

"Abbey is excited," Stacey said. She laughed as Abbey threw her arms around her legs.

"Yeah," Edwards said. "As soon as we get back to town, you can start planning." He checked his phone, reading an e-mail for a moment. "It looks like business is looking up. Sales are up thirty percent. The integrated HUD is reaching the final testing phases, and the joint chiefs are very excited. Our self-replicating body armor has just finished testing."

"It's shaping up to be a great year for EKC industries," Kennedy said smiling. "And to think, if I hadn't followed you into smoke jumper training, none of this would have happened!"

"This is the kind of trouble I could get used to," Edwards said sipping his beer, a broad smile on his face.

"Speaking of trouble," Kennedy started, grinning, "I did a little digging and found the tape from the call that sent us winging out to Erichson's in the first place. It's kinda like I figured. Mancirotti's voice was on the call."

"That makes sense," Edwards mumbled. "I saw some documents about a directed EMP weapon, and the research entries are bracketing the crash. They used us for testing."

"They got what they deserved," Stacey interrupted.

"To EKC," Bethany said raising her glass. "Here's to a long and fruitful year!"

END

Before You Go...

HELP AN AUTHOR

write a review

THANK YOU!

Share your voice and help guide other readers to these wonderful books. Even if it's only a line or two your reviews help readers discover the author's books so they can continue creating stories that you'll love. Login to your favorite retailer and leave a review. Thank you.

About the Author

Daniel Smith is from central Illinois, where he lives with his wife and four children. Smith holds a certificate of achievement in Mining Engineering.

Smith has been a life-long fan of the Science-Fiction genre, and hopes to continue his contribution to it. When he is not writing, reading or watching science fiction, Smith enjoys building furniture, doing home renovation projects and spending time with his children.